"Mrwadj see ownership as some⎯⎯⎯⎯ take something from you, it's ⎯⎯⎯⎯⎯⎯⎯ ⎯⎯⎯ it to be yours again, you take it back. All part of the game."

"Listen, Julio, I'm all for cultural diversity, but I really need the biocomputer your captain took. If I can just talk to her, explain why I need—"

Rodriguez laughed and gave his shoulder a hearty clap that almost knocked him over. "There are two problems with that plan. One, Mrwadj are creatures of impulse. Notice how they only speak in present tense? Not much sense of time, even less of consequences. To her, that computer is hers now. It won't be yours until you steal it back. And from the look of you, no offense, you couldn't steal candy from a baby."

That wasn't something David found offensive. "You said there were two problems."

"Oh, yes. We're already on our way to the Hub."

"What? You gotta turn back!"

"And wait hours or more for a new launch window? Mrwadj live in a perpetual 'now'—they hate waiting for anything. Tsshar paid handsome bribes to get a slot in the express queue. I'm sorry, David, but Tsshar's run off with more than your biocomp and your credit rod. She's stealing you as we speak."

Copyright © 2020 by Christopher L. Bennett
ISBN 978-1-951510-90-9
All rights reserved. No part of this book may be used or reproduced in any manner whatsoever without written permission except in the case of brief quotations embodied in critical articles and reviews
For information address Crossroad Press at 141 Brayden Dr., Hertford, NC 27944
A Mystique Press Production - Mystique Press is an imprint of Crossroad Press.
www.crossroadpress.com

First edition

CRIMES OF THE HUB

BOOK II OF THE HUB SERIES

BY CHRISTOPHER L. BENNETT

The contents of this volume were originally published in slightly different form as:

"Hubpoint of No Return" in *Analog Science Fiction and Fact*, Vol. CXXXVIII Nos. 5 & 6 (May/June 2018), pp. 46-64.

"...And He Built a Crooked Hub" in *Analog Science Fiction and Fact*, Vol. CXXXVIII Nos. 9 & 10 (September/October 2018), pp. 78-96.

"Hubstitute Creatures" in *Analog Science Fiction and Fact*, Vol. CXXXVIII Nos. 11 & 12 (November/December 2018), pp. 84-103.

CONTENTS

Hubpoint of No Return	1
...And He Built a Crooked Hub	45
Hubstitute Creatures	95

COUNT ONE
HUBPOINT OF NO RETURN

1

David LaMacchia strode with purpose through the bustling communications center. To either side of him was a long row of cryogenic tanks containing quantelopes, the engineered creatures whose unique entanglement properties made them a vital lifeline for the thousands of worlds of the Hub Network. Each tank had its own interface station, and the diverse sophonts who operated these were vital in their own right, for quantelopes would only reproduce the speech of living beings. And David had earned the right to count himself among their number.

With a thrill of pride and wonder, David took his station, donned his headset, and initiated his first communication of the day. As always, he marveled at the thought that he was about to interact with a being thousands of parsecs away, perhaps even in another galaxy. When the purple, short-antlered rodent in the cryotank spoke in the voice of that sophont, confirming receipt of his signal, the young human stiffened with excitement as he delivered his message:

"How do you do? This is David on behalf of the Milky Way Research Council. You've been selected to participate in a brief survey of voter opinion. We know your time is valuable, so for your participation, you'll be awarded a free eighty-two-hour vacation to the Ipqo Rosette—some local taxes and Hub processing fees may apply. If you'd like to begin the survey, please—"

The quantelope interrupted, relaying the speech heard by its entanglemate at the far end of the connection. "Survey?! How did you mate your quantelope to this bloodline? And just when I was settling down to devour my prey! Call me again and

I'll hunt you down and devour *you!*"

The quantelope let out a brief, bloodcurdling squeal and then fell silent, the connection broken. "Okay," David muttered. "One more for the hard refusal list." He signalled his quantelope to focus its attention upon a different entanglemate. "How do you do? This is David on behalf of the Milky Way Research Council—"

"You know it's all a scam, right?" Nashira Wing asked David as they carried their lunch trays through Hubstation 3742's food court. "You're using this 'miracle of communication' to cheat gullible people out of their money."

David clumsily attempted to handle his tray and a large shopping bag at the same time. "Most of them aren't that gullible. Mainly they just yell at me."

"Ah. My favorite pastime." Nashira used one hand to steady his tray, her pilot's reflexes letting her deftly balance her own in the other.

"Exactly. You've given me a thicker skin."

He smiled, and Nashira's own tray started to wobble in response. She hastened to set it down on a vacant table, then helped David guide his to a safe landing.

"I don't know why you needed a third job," she went on once they were seated. "Quantelope maintenance and the day care thing pay well enough. Hell, you don't even need to stay at the Hubcomplex to do your studies." In most of the greater galaxy, a universal basic income was guaranteed, the fruit of the Hub Network's endless wealth. But space in the Hubcomplex itself— the collection of ring habitats surrounding the unique dimensional warp through which all interstellar traffic passed—was at a premium, so it had to be earned.

"If I'd wanted to study the Hub from a distance, I would've stayed on Earth. This is where the action is. Besides, you hate *your* job, but you stay here."

"It's not like I have much choice. The Network needs all the scouts it can get, so they don't make it easy to leave."

When Nashira had arrived illegally in the Hubcomplex nine years ago, she'd been too broke to book passage to anywhere else—and she'd burned all her bridges back on Earth. She could have applied for refugee status and possibly made her way to some Network planet where she could live in modest comfort. But one stint as a refugee, when her family had fled the inundated Hong Kong for Australia, had been quite enough for her. Hub scouting had been the only available job that she hadn't found demeaning, but it was a relentlessly tedious chore—testing the vast number of untried Hub vectors one by one, never knowing where they would lead, all in the vanishingly slim hope of discovering something more profitable than empty space and less deadly than the inside of a star.

"At least there are things I'm actually good at," she went on. "Which is more that you can say."

"Well, that has to change. I tried depending on charity and it didn't work out."

There was no arguing with that. When David had first arrived in pursuit of what the college dropout laughably considered a scientific study of the Hub, Nashira had warned him that his sponsor Rynyan was a dilettante interested only in boosting his status within the decadent and charity-obsessed Sosyryn civilization, and that trusting him would inevitably get David hurt. Two months ago, she'd been proven right—which was less satisfying than she'd expected. But at least the young American had finally started to develop the cynicism he would need to survive as a member of one of the newest, least important species in the Hub Network.

Although the fact that Nashira cared at all was, perhaps, a sign that a little of David's idealism had infected her as well. This was a source of ongoing concern to Nashira, and she was monitoring the infection closely for signs of spreading. David had become an unlikely friend over the past six months, chipping away at her defenses through his relentless good nature and idealism. She had even developed a jaundiced sort of respect for his impossible dream of discovering the key to predicting new Hub vectors and thereby proving humanity's worth to the greater galaxy. In its own way, it was no more quixotic than her own vain hope of earning her way out of the scouting life— though her dream was at least mathematically possible. And

David was finally starting to grow out of his boyish innocence into a more pragmatic and frankly attractive manhood. David's core idealism seemed incurable, though, for he quickly brightened. "Anyway, there's a reason I needed the extra work. And here it is!" David removed the item from his shopping bag and placed it on the table.

Nashira stared. "You got a third job to buy a *fish?*"

That was putting it generously. The baseball-sized, bulging-eyed creature swimming languidly in the cylindrical tank resembled a fish about as much as a landfill resembled Victoria Peak. "It's not a fish," David replied. "It's an engineered aquatic biocomputer."

"Okay, but why aquatic?"

He shrugged. "All I could afford. It's refurbished."

Even as he spoke, the off-center third eye on the thing's forehead irised open and blinked sideways. The creature emitted a succession of burbly noises, then spoke in a watery, piping voice. "Language settings accepted. Earth English. Input owner information."

David cleared his throat. "Hi. David LaMacchia. I'm your owner."

"David LaMacchia." The hideous construct looked him over. "Biometrics accepted." It swung around to gaze at Nashira. "Secondary user?"

"No, thanks," Nashira said, grimacing and waving her hands. "That monstrosity's all yours. What the hell do you need a computer fish for anyway?"

"You're always saying I don't have the brains to crack the Hub's secrets," David said without rancor. "So I got an extra brain. I've had Art here bio-programmed with all available data on Hub physics and related sciences."

Nashira gave him a wary look. "Art? No, don't tell me—"

Grinning, David held up his hands as though framing a sign. "Art, a Fishy Intelligence."

"Ohh, you're dead to me, LaMacchia." He simply grinned wider.

Something warm and furry brushed Nashira's leg. Startled, she looked down to see a mammal-like creature the size of a five-year-old human, but with six limbs, brown and orange striped fur, and an almost feline aspect suggested by its large eyes, the four earlike flaps atop its head, and the slim, whiskery tentacles hanging from the corners of its muzzle.

"Mrwadj," she growled in recognition as the creature brushed against David's legs, making him chuckle. "What do *you* want?"

"Hello, little human ones," the tiny Mrwadj said, climbing up into David's lap and peering over the table edge. "What do you have for me?"

"Get away, you," Nashira warned.

"Hey, don't be rude," David said, absently stroking the Mrwadj's head. "This guy—gal—whoever is one of the first people I've met here who was friendly to a human."

"Yeah, after Rynyan," Nashira reminded him.

"I am a gal whoever," the Mrwadj said. "Tsshar Murieff, captain of the freighter *Miifu*. Who is your fish? How does it crack Hub secrets?"

"It doesn't! It won't. David, watch out. Mrwadj are infamous thieves."

"Nashira! You know better than to make racial generalizations."

"It's how they evolved. As scavengers. They pride themselves on sneakiness."

David chuckled as Tsshar clambered onto the table to peer at Art. "She's not exactly being sneaky."

"That's what worries me. What do you want, *Captain*?"

"Cracking Hub secrets sounds valuable. You need a ship? My ship takes you through the Hub. We share the secrets?"

"Thanks, but that's not necessary," David said. "Nashira's a Hub scout. We already have a ship."

"And we won't be cracking any secrets," Nashira added. "He bought this piece of second-hand flotsam with his babysitting money. There are far better things to steal around here, so go bother someone else."

"Hungry anyway," Tsshar said, leaping away over the edge of the booth. Nashira reflexively checked her pockets, her watch, and her necklace.

"Nashira, that was rude," David said. "She was just curious. I can identify with that."

"Oh, you have plenty in common," Nashira noted. "She's even eating your lunch."

Indeed, David's tray was now bereft of all but napkins and condiments. Nashira took pity and gave him half her sandwich. "Seriously, how useful can a low-end biocomp be? Does it actually know what it's talking about?"

"Let's find out." David leaned over the tank. "Art? Explain, in layperson's terms, the physics behind the Hub."

Art swam in a tight circle for a moment. "The Hub is the collective center of mass of the greater galaxy, including the dark-matter halo and all embedded stellar associations. All particles within a correlated ensemble will tend to decohere toward their most probable paths. The most probable position within an ensemble is the center of its distribution. Therefore, all particles in an ensemble tend toward its center of mass as their states mutually correlate, a tendency that manifests as gravitational attraction. The center of mass is therefore correlated with every particle within the ensemble. Normally this correlation is swamped by other particle interactions, but in an ensemble as massive as the greater galaxy, the correlation is robust enough to permit quantum tunneling between the center of mass and any other point within the ensemble."

David beamed. "There, you see? I'm already learning stuff I didn't know!"

"Assuming any of that rubbish makes sense."

"Well, ask him something yourself."

Gazing pointedly at David, Nashira leaned forward. "Hey, Fishface. Tell David here why the relationship between Hub vectors and destinations is impossible to predict."

Art's third eye blinked at her. "Identify 'David.'"

"Him!" Nashira pointed. "David LaMacchia."

It glared at her. "Biometric mismatch. You are not David LaMacchia."

"No, he is! Behind you!"

Art swum around, spotting David. "Biometrics accepted. Data mismatch. You are not behind me. Please clarify instructions."

"Just answer Nashira's question," David told him.
"Identify 'Nashira.'"
"Me! Behind you!" she cried.
Art swung around again. "Secondary user?"
"Rrr, just answer the fucking question, you severed testicle of Cthulhu!"
"Please restate question."
She restated it through clenched teeth. Mercifully, Art replied without further obstruction. "The exit coordinates associated with a given entry vector could theoretically be predicted—"
"Aha!" said David.
"—if the quantum state of every particle constituting the greater galactic system could be measured precisely. As this is effectively impossible, the degree of uncertainty remains too great to allow prediction."
David's face fell. "Oh."
"I hate to say I told you so," Nashira said, sounding a bit more apologetic than she'd intended.
"Still," David went on, rallying, "Art's just repeating what the Network already believes. I'm trying to come at it from a whole new direction, remember?"
"Then why bother with the fish?"
"So he can check my theories when I come up with them." He shrugged. "I need somebody to do the math."
Nashira scoffed. "I wouldn't trust this blob to add two and two." She tapped Art's bowl. "How about it, you stupid blowfish? What do you make of that?"
Art stared up at her. "And you are?"

Despite Nashira's urgings to get his money back, David had already grown attached to Art, insisting that only his short-term memory was at fault. After all, there was nothing David LaMacchia loved more than a lost cause. He continued to play with the piscine processor for the rest of the lunch hour, finally returning Art's tank to his shopping bag beneath the table.
"Thank you!" cried a newly familiar voice. A brown-orange streak erupted from beneath the table, carrying the bag away with it.

"David! It's Tsshar, she's stealing your stupid fish!"
"Oh, no. No, come back!" David dashed off after the thief.
"Stop! You don't know who else she's working with!"
"Art! I'm coming, Artie!"
She ran after him into Hubstation 3742's main concourse.
"David, wait! Forget the damn fish!"
"He's my responsibility!" was the last thing she heard from him before he disappeared into the crowd. Nashira pushed through the crush of travelers from dozens of species, driven by much the same sentiment. She'd never considered herself the nurturing kind, but it wasn't like anyone else was going to take care of David—and he'd just decisively demonstrated that he was not yet ready to take care of himself.

Six months ago, she couldn't have imagined going to this much trouble for anyone. Most of the people in her life were fellow Hub scouts, her rivals in the pursuit of an astronomically unlikely prize, whose success would be something to envy and resent—and whose burnout or death was common enough to discourage close relationships. Nashira certainly wouldn't miss Evdrae, a vain Druagom who had joined up three years ago and viciously resented that the younger Nashira was treated as her senior; or Stauats, an Flanx demimale who stubbornly insisted on perceiving humans as childlike primitives despite all evidence; or Jeqqun, a self-righteous Poviqq who reflexively sucked up to authority and never hesitated to get Nashira in trouble for her... creative interpretations of the rules. The closest thing she had to an ally in her scout contingent was Mansura Joumari, a fiftyish Moroccan woman who'd been on the job almost as long as Nashira. Mansura had always been a better sport than most, never actively trying to sabotage Nashira... and never holding a grudge over the few times Nashira had tried to sabotage her. But the two women had little in common and were far from close.

When it came down to it, David LaMacchia was the one person in the greater galaxy that Nashira knew would be there for her if she needed help. So saving him was an act of pure self-interest. Wasn't it? Of course it was.

Besides, she could anticipate the thief's destination. Tsshar had called herself the captain of a freighter—more likely a smuggler's ship—and Nashira knew where such a vessel would probably be docked. Taking a shortcut, she reached the docking bay just in time to see David still pursuing the tiger-striped Mrwadj as she dashed into the freighter. He was gasping for breath and staggering, but still he ran onto the gangway, oblivious to his plight. "David! Stop!" Nashira wheezed, but he vanished into the ship without hearing her—and the hatch clanged shut in his wake.

Nashira ran for the dock control station to summon help. But the ship's moorings promptly detached and it began to taxi. By the time she reached the control station, *Miifu* was already on the magnetic launch rails, decelerating against the habitat ring's rotation so that it could fall in toward the Hub. And from there, it and David could end up anywhere in nine galaxies.

She was tempted to leave the dumb kid to his fate. It would serve him right, dashing off over a useless piece of biotech. But there was no way that Nashira was going to let herself be beaten by a misbegotten cross between a tabby cat and a spider monkey.

If there was any consolation, she thought, at least David would have little to fear physically from the crew aboard that ship.

David yelped in pain as the handfoot of an enormous Hijjeg crushed him against the deck. "No stowaways!" it roared.

"I'm not a stowaway," David explained reasonably. "I'm just here to retrieve my stolen property." Due to the intense pressure on his chest, however, it came out more like "Aahhmmnnnnstooowheee! Aahhmmstrrtee-heee... mha... hhheeee!"

"Let him up, Jojjimok," came a voice he recognized as Tsshar's. "He makes it this far. He earns a chance."

The pressure mercifully relented—but the Hijjeg's idea of letting him up entailed hauling him off the deck and dangling him upside-down by his ankles. At least David could now somewhat see the ship's crew, including several Mrwadj and what looked like a human. "But we must make security," Tsshar went on. "Search him!"

The "search" consisted of several small, fuzzy, adorable

Mrwadj crawling all over his inverted form, their lightning-fast limbs unfastening his clothes and emptying his pockets. David might have been able to muster more of a protest if he hadn't been so ticklish. By the time the Hijjeg dropped him none too gently to the deck, he'd been stripped of all his possessions and clothing—although the Mrwadj crew had rejected most of the latter as "too sweaty" and tossed it aside.

As the Mrwadj scurried off to examine their prizes, David realized a strong hand was being extended to him. He looked up to see the human crewmember he'd glimpsed before—a tall, handsome, dark-skinned fellow with a thick mane of dreadlocks and a muscular torso covered only by an open, sleeveless vest. He smiled down at David. "Don't mind them," he said in a light Caribbean accent. "That's just their way of welcoming you aboard."

David accepted the offered hand and was pulled to his feet with impressive strength. "Thanks. I'm David."

"Julio Rodriguez," the man said, turning his supportive grip into a warm handshake.

"My friend tried to warn me they were thieves."

The man grinned. "So ethnocentric. Mrwadj see ownership as something to be earned. If they take something from you, it's theirs. You want it to be yours again, you take it back. All part of the game."

"I'll remember that," David said, finally releasing Julio's hand so he could retrieve his clothes. "Is that why you don't wear a shirt? Since they'd just take it anyway?"

Julio laughed. "Partly that. Partly because I'm the engineer around here and it's hot work. But mostly I just look better without one."

David couldn't argue. He'd thought Nashira Wing was the sexiest human he'd met in the Hubcomplex—though he respected her friendship and feared her wrath too much to act on it without her overt invitation—but Julio was just as stunning in his own way, and much more brazen about showing it off. David hastened to rectify his state of undress before it gave away something embarrassing.

"Listen, Julio, I'm all for cultural diversity, but I really need the biocomputer your captain took. If I can just talk to her, explain why I need—"

Rodriguez laughed and gave his shoulder a hearty clap that almost knocked him over. "There are two problems with that plan. One, Mrwadj are creatures of impulse. Notice how they only speak in present tense? Not much sense of time, even less of consequences. To her, that computer is hers now. It won't be yours until you steal it back. And from the look of you, no offense, you couldn't steal candy from a baby."

That wasn't something David found offensive. "You said there were two problems."

"Oh, yes. We're already on our way to the Hub."

"What? You gotta turn back!"

"And wait hours or more for a new launch window? Mrwadj live in a perpetual 'now'—they hate waiting for anything. Tsshar paid handsome bribes to get a slot in the express queue. I'm sorry, David, but Tsshar's run off with more than your biocomp and your credit rod. She's stealing you as we speak."

2

Nashira got no help from the dock supervisors; most likely Captain Murieff paid handsomely for their cooperation. So she hastened to the Hubstation's central office—the middle ground between the concourse, where travelers from dozens of species wended their way toward known, safe, civilized destinations, and the staging area for the scouts who risked their lives and sanity in hopes of adding new destinations to the list. With the station manager's permission, she could use her scout clearance to cut through the gridlock and possibly beat *Miifu* to the Hub.

"Zilior, I need to talk to—" Nashira pulled up short at the sight of the sophont behind the office desk. Rather than the gaunt, four-armed figure of the Jiodeyn female who'd been acting as interim manager for the past two months, she beheld a tall, leonine-featured biped with tawny skin and a mane of golden feathers cascading down his back. That mane was perhaps a bit less lush and well-groomed than she remembered, but the shock of recognition was undiminished. "Rynyan?!"

Rynyan Zynara ad Surynyyyyyy'a shot to his feet and spread his arms effusively as he strode toward her. "Nashira! Oh, what a welcome sight you are after so long apart! Come, let me embrace you!"

"Fat chance!" Reflexes honed over years of fending off drunks in bars kicked in, and Rynyan ended up slammed into the wall. *Damn, that felt good,* thought Nashira. *Why didn't I do that ages ago?*

But Rynyan recovered easily, both body and spirit unbroken. "Ohh, my dear friend, you misunderstand my intentions. I was merely pleased to see a friendly face once again!"

She grudgingly admitted to herself that she may have overreacted. His frequent sexual advances had never gone beyond the verbal, or she *would* have tossed him into a wall long before now.

"Oh, Nashira, you don't know how it's been for me." Rynyan flopped melodramatically onto the office couch. "Ever since the... complications with that charity scandal, my reputation has taken a terrible blow."

"Yeah, right. I saw the news afterward. You took all the credit for exposing the conspiracy and came out smelling like a rose."

It had been Rynyan's arrogance that had enabled the conspiracy in the first place, when a lover of his, Hwaieur Aytriaew, had tricked him into helping her smuggle bioweapons past Hub customs under the pretext of cutting red tape for charity shipments. Aytriaew had even roped Nashira in as her pilot, making the Hub scout an unwitting accomplice until Nashira had figured out her scam and talked Rynyan into exposing it.

"I tried to give you the credit, truly. It's just that the press loves me so much that they wouldn't believe me. But you know how celebrity is."

"Yeah, absolutely, that's something I would know," she deadpanned.

"Well, reality is a different matter, you understand. Once the initial flush of fame and praise wore off, people began to question my judgment regarding how I donated my wealth. They didn't want people to suspect their intentions as well. So I've become a pariah, Nashira. No one will accept my charity! The past few weeks have been so... so..."

"Humiliating?"

"*Boring!* I've simply had nothing to do with my time! Well, plenty of sex, of course, but even that can get boring when there's nothing else to do. I needed to be useful somehow! Giving of myself to others is my purpose in life. But nobody will accept my services as charity, so I've had no choice but to..." He shuddered. "To *sell* them. Can you imagine? Being *paid* money instead of giving it away! It's so demeaning. I don't know how you stand it."

"Oh, cue the violins."

"No, I think you've shown me quite enough violence, Nashira. But you're right—I shouldn't complain. I deserve it all." He lowered his head. "I let myself be tricked into facilitating the smuggling of a bioweapon. My mistakes made many people suffer. It's only fitting that I should suffer in return. Why, it's positively noble. How can I do less?"

Oh, hell, Nashira thought. *Even when he's guilt-ridden, he's full of himself.*

Rynyan rose and clasped his tapered fingers before him. "And as part of my penance, my journey through humility, I've re-examined my past behavior. And I realize that it was inappropriate to continue my sexual invitations after you'd made your refusal clear. If, for whatever incomprehensible reason, you insist on denying yourself the supreme pleasures I could bestow upon you... why, then I must respect your choice. However much I pity you for what you're missing, it is not about me."

Was there genuine contrition beneath that morass of self-congratulatory bombast? He was still deeply clueless, but if there was a chance he'd actually halt his advances, then that was a non-consummation devoutly to be wished. "Well. That's... very mature of you, Rynyan. And it's... it's the one thing I've ever truly wanted you to give me. It's not easy for a human in the Network to have her choices respected—even by people who think they're doing her favors by telling her she's wrong."

Rynyan, to his credit, seemed to make a genuine effort to parse that. "My. I hadn't realized... Well. Yes. Definitely, then. You neither want nor need my assistance in the erotic arena, and so I will no longer offer it." He extended his hand.

"Deal," she said, accepting the handshake.

"Excellent."

"Rynyan?"

"Yes, Nashira?"

"I need your assistance."

"*Yes!* What a relief! Let's see, the couch seems a bit small..." She slapped his hand away. "No, not for that!"

"Oh. Oh, dear. Sorry, I still need to work on this, obviously..."

"Rynyan! David's in trouble!"

"David?! *My* David? He needs my help again?" He tilted his head back and shook his fists in the air. "Yes! I knew this day would come!"

"Rynyan!"

"Right. Not about my needs. I'm trying, I am. Now, what can I do to help dear David?"

Nashira hastily explained the situation. "So if I can just get clearance to launch the *Entropy* and go after them—"

"Of course. You are more than welcome to take out your Hubdiver any time you want."

"Great." She turned for the door.

"A-a-a-s soon as its overhaul is complete."

She spun back. "Overhaul?"

Rynyan fidgeted with his mane. "Well, I wanted to do something really generous for you. You were always complaining about how, well, entropic the *Starship Entropy* was, so I ordered a full overhaul. You'll love it, really, I'm putting in all the newest upgrades—"

"How... long?"

"It shouldn't be more than another, oh, four days."

Nashira threw up her hands. Within an hour, David could be anywhere in the greater galaxy. In one afternoon, she'd lost David and regained Rynyan. What else could go wrong today?

David soon found that Tsshar had permitted him the run of the ship. Apparently he was being challenged to find Art and his other possessions, and to steal them back if he could. But his search turned up no sign of the cyber-organism. A ship like this no doubt had many hidey-holes, and once David ruled out *Millennium Falcon*-style compartments under the deck plates, that exhausted his knowledge of space smuggling techniques.

The crew was hardly any help. Tsshar was happy to let David search, but she had no intention of making it easy. The other Mrwadj were largely indifferent. Julio was friendly but unwilling to cross his captain. And Jojjimok, the Hijjeg crewmember, watched David's every move, ready to pounce at the slightest transgression—and the prospect of being pounced on by a two-meter-wide, aggressively aromatic mountain of flesh was not particularly appealing even to an open-minded fellow like David.

In time, Julio escorted David to *Miifu*'s bridge at the captain's invitation. On arrival, he saw that the ship was within the Shell, the launch machinery aligning it for its impending dive. The Hub itself was directly before them, and yet, as always, his eyes were unable to bring that eerie dimensional pucker into focus. "Where are we going?" David asked.

Julio grinned in response. "Get a load of this."

A moment later, they plunged into the center of all things...

...then *Miifu*'s reverse thrusters fired hard to stop the ship from smashing into a wall. David felt the ship's nanofog tighten around him to cushion the thrust, and Julio's strong grip on his arm provided extra bracing. The others had all braced themselves in advance.

Once the nanofog's hold softened, David stepped forward... and realized he had weight. Genuine weight, not the convenient simulacrum that nanofog provided. They were somewhere with gravity—and within walls. Gazing out the port, David saw the interior of an enormous cylindrical chamber like a roofed stadium. "I don't understand. You can't keep a Hubpoint inside a building. The planet's rotation would whisk it away in seconds. You could park a space station around one, but you'd have to spin it to get gravity."

"You look at the wrong thing," Tsshar told him. "Come out—take a better look."

David followed the captain and her crew down the open gangway to the floor—or deck—of the structure they occupied. He quickly saw that, although the path between the Hubpoint and the wall had been cleared to provide a safe landing strip, the rest of the echoing chamber was filled with eclectic artifacts. Some were clearly sculptures and other artwork; some were undeniably technological; most could've been either as far as David could tell. Many were neatly arranged within the space, while others were jammed in randomly, as if shoved aside to make the landing strip. There were gaps in the pattern, as if items had been removed.

Spotting a plaque on one artifact, David moved in for a closer look. He blinked, waiting for his translator implant to kick in. But nothing happened. "What's wrong? I can't read it."

"None of us can," said Julio, who'd been hanging close to him while the others ranged about the chamber. Jojjimok was already hefting a large artifact in two of his outer armlegs, using his other two and the four stubbier legs underneath his body to propel him forward. Tsshar darted around, examining multiple artifacts, while her crew scattered to parts unknown.

"But our implants are programmed with every language in the Network."

"That's right." Julio's smile widened.

The implications finally sank in. "You found a non-Network civilization?" *If only Nashira were here*, he thought. His friend dreamed of discovering something priceless like this, staking a claim, and becoming rich enough to get out of the scouting life. But how did *Miifu*'s crew find this place if a Hub scout hadn't already discovered and claimed it?

"Look around," said Julio. "Does this look like one civilization to you?"

Indeed, the mix of designs was dizzyingly diverse. Many artworks seemed to depict living beings, but ones so radically dissimilar that they were unlikely to have evolved on the same planet. "But how can there be stuff from multiple species here if they aren't part of the Hub Network?" His eyes widened. "Unless... Do they have a faster-than-light drive?"

Julio laughed. "Ohh, are you on the wrong track!"

Tsshar hopped onto David's shoulder, startling him. "Not *the* Hub Network. *A* Hub network. Come, come and see." She leapt off and scampered toward a ramp that rose along the outer wall. Julio followed, clasping David's arm to draw him forward.

As they ascended the ramp, David felt a deep vibration coming from the wall. "Are we in some kind of spaceship?"

"Something like that," Julio said.

They climbed through multiple levels housing smaller artifacts, finally reaching a control booth atop the structure. Its consoles were designed for alien digits and labeled in unreadable script, but a Network-issue portable workstation rested atop one console with a jury-rigged hard connection to it, and some of the controls were adorned with sticky notes bearing writing in a recognizable Network script.

Yet words were unnecessary. The view out the side ports spoke volumes. They were in a raised dome near the edge of the cylindrical structure, just inside a very thick toroidal rim. Protrusions that looked like reaction control thrusters poked out at various places along that rim. Beyond was the bare black of intergalactic space, broken only by the faint haze of a distant dwarf galaxy or two.

"I don't understand. We're in space, but we have weight. Are we moving? Have we left the Hubpoint behind?" His eyes widened. "Are we trapped here? I got trapped like that once..."

"No, nothing like that," Julio said. "We'd have had to know exactly when it passed through the Hubpoint. And with the traffic around the Shell, we could never have timed it so exactly, could we?"

David frowned. "So how can we have gravity?"

"Look here." Tsshar activated the portable workstation. On its screen, a wireframe graphic of the structure appeared in blue. The entire multilevel facility was ringed by a series of thick, helical conduits, each helix looped into a single broad ring, with several rings stacked atop each other. Within the heart of the structure was a red dot indicating the position of the Hubpoint.

Julio gestured at the graphic. "Running through those conduits is a hyperdense, high-velocity superfluid. Zero friction, like superconductivity for mass, so it never slows down, never stops. The flow pattern creates a gravitomagnetic field perpendicular to the ring, like how an electric current in a loop creates a magnetic field. It's basically what human science calls a Forward catapult."

David frowned. "Don't all catapults go forward?"

Julio laughed. "*Robert* Forward. A physicist from about a century ago. He designed it as a kind of mass driver, a theoretical way to launch spaceships. But you can also build a station inside one and have artificial gravity. Long as we're inside the loop, we feel weight."

"So more of a Downward catapult." Julio just laughed

louder. "It's amazing," David went on. "But why go to all the trouble?"

"Many artifacts here come from planets," Tsshar elaborated. "Meant to be in gravity. Fountains, pendulums, games with rolling balls, art with draped cords and fabrics. So they make gravity."

"Why haven't I heard of a technology like this before?"

"Hard to make, not too safe," Tsshar said. "All that mass racing around so fast—what if something breaks? Awful mess. Lots of dying. Not worth the trouble when you have nanofog."

This was hardly reassuring to David, but Julio took pity on him. "Not to worry. Whoever built this archive found a way to make it stable. That superfluid has kept on circulating for over two hundred thousand years."

"Two hundred thousand? But the Dosperhag only discovered the Hub sixteen thousand years ago!"

"And the galaxy's thirteen billion years old. You really think nobody else found the Hub in all that time?"

David took that in. "So if there was an earlier Hub civilization… what happened to them?"

"We don't know," Tsshar said. "But whatever makes them go away, someone knows it's coming. Someone who gathers its treasures, stores them out here where nothing disturbs them. No stars tug the archive too far off the Hubpoint, no asteroids puncture the mass conduits, no supernovas burn out the computers. So it's here to be owned again—by someone clever enough to take it."

"Don't you mean lucky?" David challenged. "There's no way you found this Hubpoint except by chance."

"I don't find it. A Hub scout finds it. Not the original Hubpoint, but close enough to reach the archive in his ship. He sees how valuable it is. Revolutionary. World-changing. Not just the one new world every scout dreams to find—hundreds. The legacy of a whole Hub network. Of course that's too valuable to share. Of course he keeps the find to himself." She used a few arms to gesture toward the RCS modules. "He thrusts the archive here, parks it around the Hubpoint. Plans to come back at leisure, smuggle out artifacts bit by bit, get rich. Clever plan."

"So how'd you find out?"

"Scouting is dangerous. Dive into a star, dive into a planet. The scout doesn't come back one day. So sad. But his stuff needs a good home, so I give it one. I find his journal. I make his plan mine, his riches mine."

"In tribute to his memory, I suppose."

"Of course. Always honor a worthy thief." Tsshar's four half-moon earflaps folded back. "But not bit by bit. Too inefficient. We clean the place out."

"But that's grave robbing! Tsshar, all this—it belongs in a museum!" Han Solo hadn't helped him, but maybe Indiana Jones could.

"It's in a museum. But nobody can see it. We're taking it out so it can breathe again."

Julio shrugged. "Remember who you're talking to, David. To a Mrwadj, 'museum' means 'motherlode.' But don't worry—we're fully documenting it all in situ. Some archaeologist may pay well for that data."

David wasn't reassured. This was too revolutionary a find to keep secret. But it wouldn't be easy to convince a crew of thieves to stop thieving. Maybe if he bided his time and got to know these people better, he could connect with them and help them see the error of their ways.

Or he could find a way to call Nashira so she could come kick their butts.

So for now, he changed the subject. "There's one more thing I don't get. Art—my biocomputer. I only had him programmed with information about Hub physics. Why did you think he'd be useful here?"

"I don't think your fish is useful," Tsshar said. "Your fish is bait. I think you're useful."

"For what?"

Tsshar blinked up at him with her wide, adorable eyes. "This stuff is heavy. Somebody has to carry it into the ship."

3

David laded artifacts until he ached all over, but even once *Miifu* was full, his work was not yet done. Tsshar left David, Julio, and Jojjimok behind to ready more artifacts for transfer while she took the freighter back through the Hub to unload. In case of emergency, she left a mobile quantelope tank behind, then used the shipboard 'lopes to contact the Hub and request the laser beam that would reopen the Hubpoint. There was no need to vent the atmosphere first, since only an object whose vector of motion was aligned with the beam and equal in velocity to the entry vector would tunnel through the Hubpoint. At most, only a few air molecules might pass through.

During a meal break, David managed to slip away to the control room, hoping to get a look at its computer files and find out whether the earlier Hub-based civilization had found the key to the Hub's physics. Maybe they had abandoned the Hub because they'd invented a better FTL drive. True, he and the computer would have no languages in common, but the scout who'd left those sticky notes must have deciphered enough to allow a starting point. Maybe the portable workstation could serve as a translator.

But the workstation used unfamiliar software, and David's language implant could only do so much with bad handwriting. He found that if he leaned in close enough to the sticky notes, the implant could make a reasonable guess at the letters. But the console had evidently been made for a long-limbed species, and some of the notes were hard to reach. Absently, David reached out and tugged one free to bring it closer. "Okay, that says 'air pressure'... or is it 'fuel pressure'?" Remembering a similar-looking note to his upper left, he reached out and snagged it so he could compare them side by side.

"What are you doing?"

It was Julio. Startled, David spun and straightened, hiding the two notes behind his back. "I was just... looking for an inventory list. You know, to help us, um, steal stuff more efficiently." He leaned back, trying to look casual as he reached blindly to try to put one of the notes back in place.

"Is that a sticky note stuck to your left arm?" Julio asked.

"What? No," David said, starting to become aware of the sensation of a sticky note stuck to his left arm.

"Yes, there is! Right there!" David slapped his right hand over the note before Julio could get a better look at it. "And there's another one! There, on your elbow!" David moved his hand to cover his left elbow, exposing the note on his arm and dropping the crumpled one he'd had in his hand. "Oh, David, what have you done? We need those!"

"It's all right," David insisted, gathering up the notes. "I'll put them back, don't worry."

"Do you remember where they went?"

"Of course. They're all clearly color-coded."

"They're all the same color!"

"Maybe to human eyes."

"And what do you think you are?"

"Open to alternative points of view."

"Just put the damn notes back!"

David concentrated, visualizing their placement in his memory. Yes, the fuel pressure tag went in the upper right, over that squiggly blue symbol... or was it under the squiggly blue symbol? Or was that the air pressure tag?

"You're just guessing!" Julio said after a few hesitant tries.

"I'm trusting my instincts! Now, this one got stuck to my elbow when I spun, so it had to be from the middle here..."

"That's the one that was in your hand!"

"I can tell my hand from my elbow, Julio."

"It has your fingerprints on it in jelly!"

"Oh, good point."

"Look, maybe the workstation has a key." Julio tried

searching it, but soon found that the Hub scout who'd installed it had either encrypted the files or just been a sloppy note taker.

Finally, using a mix of memory and deductive logic—and perhaps just a touch of educated guessing—they had the notes back in what David was fairly convinced was the correct arrangement. "Now I just have to access the archive's database," David said.

"Are you sure that's wise?"

"The notes can't be that far off." David hit the computer activation control.

The archive jerked and rumbled as the thrusters fired. David lost his balance and went down in a tangle of limbs with Julio. "Oh. *That's* the computer panel over there!"

"Get off!" They needed several moments to untangle their limbs and regain their feet, after which Julio stared in alarm at the workstation graphic. "Oh, no. The archive's starting to move!"

"Don't worry, I'll shut them off." David found the thruster control and hit it again. The thrusters doubled their intensity. David fell over again, but Julio dodged and David fell unimpeded to the deck. This time he was ready for it, so he rolled back easily to his feet. "That's weird." He tried it one more time. The thrusters doubled again and David reeled.

"Not that one!" Julio shoved past him, sending him to the deck once more, and scanned the panel. "These. They must be paired, increase and decrease." He hit the counterpart control three times. Finally the thrust cut off.

"Oh, good," David said, regaining his feet and rubbing his backside. "We're okay now."

"Are you kidding? We're drifting!"

"There's nothing out here to hit."

Julio grabbed the front of his shirt, pointing toward the workstation. "The Hubpoint, you idiot!" On the screen, the red dot representing the Hubpoint was drifting sideways within the archive wireframe. "We have to stop moving before we drift past it!"

"Oh!" They wasted precious moments deciphering which controls were for the opposing thrusters. "These! It must be."

Bracing himself, David struck the control. Instead of the opposing thrusters, the perpendicular thrusters fired. The Hubpoint's drifting path started to curve.

"No! Shut them off!"

He hit the button again, doubling the thrust, then caught himself and hit the paired control twice. "Sorry."

"It must be this one," Julio said. This time, the correct thruster fired, slowing the archive's drift. "But it's still drifting sideways!" He pointed David to the proper controls. "There. No longer a burn than before!"

With trial and error, they managed to cancel out the drift, overcompensate, correct, and eventually bring the structure to a relative halt once more. "There," David sighed.

Julio swallowed and pointed to the screen. "Not there." The Hubpoint was still inside the archive, all right, but ensconced within one of the superfluid conduits. "We have to reverse thrust, get it back inside the main vault."

"Right." He scanned the panel. "It should be... this one."

Julio caught his hand and gave his head a warning shake. "It's *this* one!" He pressed it... and nothing happened.

"What? No, no..." The burly engineer tested the other thruster controls. None gave more than a brief fizzle before dying out. "What's the fuel pressure gauge read?"

David checked. "Umm, nominal. But... uh-oh. The air pressure reads zero. Did we spring a leak?"

Julio stared. "You got the labels backward, damn it! We're out of thruster fuel!"

"You mean... the Hubpoint is stuck inside the wall?"

"Inside a million tons of hyperdense superfluid, and *that's* inside dozens of meters of piping and shielding strong enough to contain it. We don't have a prayer of getting to it, and if *Miifu* dives back through the Hubpoint, it'll be crushed in an instant." Julio slumped. *"Now* we're trapped."

Rynyan's new role as Hubstation manager gave him the authority to impound and search *Miifu* as soon as it returned through the Hub, and to allow Nashira to accompany the search team. But David was nowhere on board. "Where is he?" Rynyan demanded as he and Nashira questioned Tsshar Murieff in her quarters. "I'll order this ship dismantled if that's what it takes to find him!"

"No need," the diminutive captain said breezily. "Little human stays behind to help out."

"Stays behind where?" Nashira demanded, looming over her. "We checked the dive logs. You took a junk vector. Scout report says it's deep intergalactic, nothing for kiloparsecs. So where did you leave him?" she went on through clenched teeth. "Empty space?"

The captain reacted with amusement. "Why would I take his life, silly? I can't keep it, he can't take it back. What's the point?"

Further questioning proved fruitless. Finally, Nashira asked Rynyan to assign a security patrol to follow the reputed junk vector and discover what was really on the other side. "Absolutely," Rynyan agreed. "And I'm going with them."

"What? You're the manager now. You can't just walk out whenever you want."

"But David's in trouble! I have to show him he can still depend on me."

"So you swoop in, the conquering hero, and he trusts you again?" She shook her head. "Doesn't work that way. David won't trust you until you prove you can make a decision that's not about you, or about what other people think of you. Until you show you can help people just for their sake, not yours." She fidgeted. "As far as I can understand that cornfed idealism of his, anyway."

Rynyan's face bore the most contrite expression she'd ever seen on a Sosyryn. "You understand him better than I ever have, my dear. I hope you know how much I appreciate your mind as well as your sleek and supple—"

"Stop," she interrupted. "Go back seven words and try again."

"Right. Sorry. What I mean to say is… You're right, I shouldn't go. But I can ask you to go in my place."

Nashira blinked. "Saves me the trouble of browbeating you into it. Don't worry, I'll bring him back in one piece. Two at most."

"I know you will, Nashira. You've looked out for him so

well, even though it didn't gain you any status. I know I can trust you to keep our David safe."

It took Nashira a moment to sort through the cognitive dissonance of a compliment from Rynyan that didn't make her feel like a piece of meat. "Right," she finally said, turning to leave.

But a gray-striped Mrwadj dashed into the room and whispered in Captain Murieff's ear. A moment later, Tsshar addressed Nashira. "Might want to hold off on that Hub dive, little human. You end up a lot more little if you try."

4

Tsshar led them to Miifu's quantelope tank, where one of the 'lopes relayed the voice of her engineer as he explained the plight that David—of course it was David—had gotten them into. Nashira reeled from the realization of how close she'd come to death. If she'd emerged inside the archive's superfluid rings, she and her ship would have been crushed to atoms in an instant. That was a risk she took every time she dove on an untried vector, and she had learned to live with it—but always with the understanding that if she emerged inside a star or planet, she'd never know she'd died. Being aware of such a close call was much more frightening. *Oh, David, you idiot!*

"Don't worry, David," Rynyan insisted, crouching down to speak face-to-face with the quantelope in urgent tones. "We'll get you out of there safely, you can be sure of that."

The purple cryo-rodent blinked back dumbly with its limpid dark eyes. But the words it spoke in David's voice were rather less innocent. "Rynyan? What the hell are you doing there? I told you we were done."

Nashira sighed. "David, he's the new station manager. I know, it's... just roll with it. The important thing is to get that Hubpoint back inside. Now, are you sure the thrusters are depleted? Any chance they're just on a maintenance cycle?"

The quantelope switched voices to that of the engineer, Julio Rodriguez. "I'm sure. It looks like the scout who moved the archive used up most of the fuel reserves. He never refueled because he didn't know how... and didn't expect to move it again anyway."

"How about airlocks? If you vent atmosphere—"

"The Forward rings are far too massive. Blowing the air

would barely budge us. And all the suits and reserve tanks are back in the ship with you."

"Gyros? If you could rotate clear of the Hubpoint, we could send a ship through outside and board you."

"The gyro effect from all that hyperdense, spinning mass is so strong that nothing we've got could budge our axis. Even all the crazy thrusting we did had no effect on it."

David's voice cut in. "What if you opened the Hubpoint? Wouldn't the superfluid, I dunno, spill out?"

Nashira sighed. "You know it doesn't work that way, kid. The superfluid's vector won't match. At most a couple of stray particles might pop out." She scoffed. "Hell, I *wish* it worked that way. Then if we connected inside a star or planet, we'd get a gush of high-density matter out through the Hub, and we'd know it wasn't safe to dive there."

"Although," Rynyan pointed out, "that would do rather unsalutary things to the Shell, wouldn't it?"

"Yeah, shame, that." Nashira snickered.

"So what *can* we do?" the quantelope asked in David's plaintive voice.

No answer was forthcoming. "I need to notify the authorities," Rynyan said after a moment. "The experts can work out a solution."

"No," Tsshar objected. "The archive is ours. No one else knows." She hissed a command, and more Mrwadj appeared at the entrances, carrying weapons.

Nashira scoffed. "Are you kidding? I could step on you lot before you could shoot me."

"Don't be rash, Nashira," Rynyan said. "There's always a way to get everyone what they want. Captain Murieff, you could just file a claim on the archive. Then you'd control access to it and the disposition of its resources."

Tsshar scowled in distaste. "Own legally? Not by guile or skill? Why even bother?"

David's voice cut in. "You got the Hub scout's journal by guile, right? Isn't that close enough?"

"Captain," Julio added, "we can't hold out here more than a day or two."

"Okay," Tsshar said. "No, wait. Not okay. Or..." Her ears folded back. "Hate deciding. Rather just act."

Nashira leaned in to her. "What's to decide, Tsshar? You like a challenge, right? To take things others are trying to keep from you?"

"Of course!"

"Well, the universe is trying to keep you from getting your crew back. Are you gonna let it get away with that?"

"No!" Tsshar replied without a second's deliberation. "I claim the vector. First step in the plan. We steal my crew back, yes! Take that, stupid universe!"

The Mrwadj dashed out with Rynyan to handle the filing. The guards melted away from the doors. But Nashira stayed by the tank. "David? It'll be okay. We're working the problem. The experts'll figure something out." There was an uncharacteristic silence from the other end. "David?"

"I know you'll do everything you can, Nashira. But... can we trust Rynyan? What if he's still just out for himself?"

She was slow to answer. "Rynyan is... He's a whole lot of things, David. But... he *thinks* he means well. And he really wants to win your trust back. He won't abandon you." Of all the incredible things happening today, hearing herself defend Rynyan topped the list.

"Just... keep an eye on him, okay? I'll be fine here. I'm making new friends. But you're the one I trust to get us out of here."

Nashira blinked and rubbed moisture from her eyes as she left the comm shack. *Damn Mrwadj fur flying everywhere. Must be allergic.*

Jojjimok reacted quite badly to the news that he and the two humans were stranded on the archive. David had his hands full trying to calm the howling behemoth.

"There, there," he cooed, stroking the squishy flab of one of Jojjimok's armlegs and doing his best to endure the foghorn volume of his wails and the overpowering aroma of Hijjeg panic sweat. "It'll be okay. The experts are doing everything they can. Don't worry."

He continued in that vein until the massive creature finally sobbed himself to sleep, curled in a fetal position against the curved wall of the archive. It was with relief that David finally got some distance so he could breathe freely once again.

"You're good with him." Julio leaned against the wall nearby, muscular arms crossed over his bare chest. "Generally it takes at least three of us to calm the big guy down."

David shrugged. "It's the least I can do. After all, it's kind of my fault we're in this mess."

"Oh, it is absolutely and entirely your fault."

"So… you're still mad at me?"

Julio glanced over at Jojjimok. "No, I guess not. If we're gonna spend the last few days of our lives together, we might as well get along."

"Don't give up, Julio. They'll think of something."

"I've been thinking too, you know." He tapped his head. "I'm not just a pretty face. Ph.D. in engineering and B.S. in physics from UWI St. Augustine, back home in Trinidad."

"Wow. Then how'd you end up as a thief?"

Julio shrugged. "You know the drill. Earth's the most backward world in the Network. I came out here hoping to learn the secrets of the universe, but even with all my education, I could barely get a job. At least as a thief, I get to use my wits, be creative." He sighed. "But I can't think of a way out of this. Even if they fired a hot enough laser through the Hubpoint to break down the superfluidity of the working mass, we'd just lose gravity once it finally ground to a halt. It'd still be too dense for us to move the station or break through to the Hubpoint. And there's no way to create a stable void within such a dense fluid." His dreads waved as he shook his head. "There's just no way out of this."

David smiled. "Believe it or not, I've been trapped on the wrong side of a Hubpoint before. That time we didn't even have live quantelopes to call for help. We thought we'd be trapped forever. But then we were rescued."

"Really? How?"

His mood fell. "By luck, really. Rynyan had already stolen the claim out from under Nashira before the 'lopes died. His greed saved us by accident, and he took the credit. Now he's the one in charge of getting us out of this." He shook his head. "Maybe I'm fooling myself. Maybe we are stuck here."

"Hey. Don't you go pessimist on me. I could use some hope right now, even if it's blind."

David held the other man's eyes for a moment. "You're right. We can't give up. Maybe... maybe there's an answer on this end. I mean, these people came from a different Hub civilization. They may have known things we don't. Like a way to calculate new Hubpoints."

Julio's face grew skeptical. "You really believe that garbage?"

"It's part of why I'm trying to solve that problem. So many people's lives would be better if we could open Hubpoints wherever we wanted."

"If the archivists knew how to open Hubpoints anywhere, why go to so much trouble to park this thing where it wouldn't be perturbed too far off the Hubpoint?"

"But why even park it there if they didn't think future civilizations could find it?"

Julio furrowed his brow. "Hold on... Maybe you are onto something. The original Hubpoint, the one this archive used to be parked around before it drifted here. The archivists' civilization must've had a record of its coordinates. Maybe there's something here with that information—either in the computer or in one of the artifacts. If we could get that vector, the Hub could send a ship through to the original Hubpoint! It should be close enough that a ship can still reach us in time."

David beamed. "That's a great idea! Let's start looking."

"Oh... and we'd better try to wake up Jojjimok. All hands on deck."

"'Try'?"

"Assuming he hasn't gone into defensive hibernation already. Come on, we'd better hurry..."

"Good news!" Rynyan told the stranded personnel over the quantelope link, while Nashira and Tsshar stood by. "Our experts have a plan. They want to send a large quantity of antimatter through the Hub. The blast should tear open the mass conduits and thrust the archive off the Hubpoint!"

"Are they crazy?" Julio's voice demanded, though the quantelope relaying it continued munching placidly on its roughage. "The Hubpoint's closer to the inner wall than the outer hull. It's more likely to blast inward and kill us all!"

"They've looked over the specs Captain Murieff provided," Rynyan went on. "They theorize that the inner wall is armored to protect the interior from accidental breaches. They believe the bulk of the force will be directed outward."

"And how sure are they of that?" Julio demanded.

"Well over fifty percent! At least fifty-seven!"

"No! No way are we betting our lives on the flip of a coin!"

"There may be a better way," David said. He filled them in on their search for an artifact containing the archive's Hub vector. "We haven't found anything here so far, but maybe something the crew took back with them has what we need. So you should search the ship too."

"Great idea," Nashira said. But her mind reeled at possibilities beyond rescuing David.

"No good," Tsshar hastened to put in. "We check inventory. We find nothing here."

"But you weren't looking for this," David replied. "You could've missed something."

"He's right, Captain," said Rynyan. "It's worth taking a careful look. If we don't, that leaves the antimatter bomb."

"And even if that didn't kill us," Julio reminded her, "it could still destroy a lot of artifacts."

Tsshar's tentacles twitched. "Okay. We look. You look. Everybody look."

Nashira thought the captain was in an awful hurry to leave the quantelope shack. She slipped out after Tsshar, treading softly.

She found the tiger-striped Mrwadj in a storage hold, clasping a prism-like object and dithering over a hidden compartment that lay open, as though trying to decide whether to stash the object. It was easy for Nashira to guess what it was. "You *do* have a list!" she accused, stepping forward.

Tsshar moved swiftly to hide the prism, but Nashira's urgency and longer limbs drove her faster, and she caught the door of the cache before it could lock shut. Retrieving the prism, she looked it over. All six of its long faces were covered in fine writing. Much of it was gibberish to her translator implant, but the rest resolved before her eyes into numerical sequences. There were only so many ways of writing numbers, and though these symbols were alien, their patterns must have matched a numerical scheme used in the Network. Nashira recognized them as angular coordinates and a velocity term. "Hub vectors! Hundreds of them!" Tilting the prism revealed even deeper layers of text. "Thousands!" She glared at Tsshar. "You knew you had this! You could've saved them already!"

"Doesn't work," the Mrwadj said. "Too many numbers. No way to know which is the archive."

"Then why were you so torn over hiding this thing?" Kneeling to look the captain in the eyes, Nashira softened her tone. "You believe this can save your crew. So you have to know which vector it is. How? Did you find it somewhere else in the archive? Somewhere David and your people can find?"

Tsshar fidgeted, pawing at the prism. "Only a fragment. Need this to complete it. If they could find, I don't need to decide. I hate deciding."

"I get why you don't want to give this away," Nashira said. "Most Hub scouts go their whole careers without finding anything more than empty space. But these..." She gazed raptly into the prism's depths. "They wouldn't have written these down if they weren't good vectors. These are addresses for star systems, habitable worlds the Network doesn't know about!"

"Not good in here-time. Hubpoints drift. Worlds move far away."

"But some places have less drift than others. Like the archive. A lot of these places could still be within days' or weeks' travel of their Hubpoints." She couldn't help laughing—and weeping. "I've spent nine years hoping to find just one good vector, and I could be holding dozens, hundreds in my hands right now."

"Must take it to have it," Tsshar warned, her hackles raised. "I call the crew. More of us than you."

Nashira shook herself, remembering the more immediate stakes. "Look, this isn't about you or me. It's about saving our friends. We have to tell them the vector."

Tsshar gestured toward the prism. "And lose this? Lose all it could give us?"

The Hub scout had to admit that if she had to choose between David's life and the opportunities this prism offered, she'd have as hard a time deciding as Tsshar. But another option occurred to her. "We can have both. We can say we found the archive vector somewhere else. Forge it on one of the other artifacts. And I'll keep quiet about the rest of this list."

Tsshar studied her. "In exchange for?"

Now they were speaking the same language. "You let me search these vectors instead of you. I put in the claim on any find, we split the profits." Tsshar hesitated. "Look, it benefits you too! A freighter testing unknown vectors would draw attention. But it's my job. Nobody'd get suspicious."

"A Hub scout who keeps finding good stuff looks suspicious."

"I just need one big score, enough to get out of the life. Then you can find another scout to take over."

"Hm. Good plan. Plus we get my crew back."

Nashira shook herself. "Yeah. Right. Them."

They turned... and found Rynyan blocking the exit, his arms crossed sternly. "Shame on you, Nashira!" He strode forward and took the prism from her grasp. "Thinking of personal gain in the face of all this artifact offers."

"No, you don't understand. I was going to—"

"Why, this is my ticket to redemption!" he went on, cradling the prism lovingly. "Once I share these addresses with the Network... all the wealth I'll give them freely... it'll be the greatest charitable act in Sosyryn history! Nobody will turn away my support anymore!" By the time he finished, he was already out the door, talking mainly to himself.

Nashira followed, Tsshar scampering after her. "Wait, Rynyan! What about David?"

"Right," the Mrwadj piped up, darting in front of the much taller Sosyryn. "I don't tell the right vector if you give away the list."

"You're bluffing," Rynyan replied. "You said you wouldn't take lives."

"I don't take them. Little human traps them all. You steal the list. Anything happens to their lives, that's not from me." She groomed herself idly. "They die? So sad. But people die. I can steal more crew."

Nashira grabbed Rynyan's arm. "I think she's serious. She won't give us that address if you go public with the list."

"But it's on here somewhere! We can organize a massive search, test every vector here."

"That could take weeks! They don't have enough food!"

"Then we'll try the antimatter option."

"Which has a forty-three percent chance of killing them! Rynyan, Tsshar's vector is a sure thing."

"At what cost to the Network? Nashira," Rynyan urged, "I'm trying to do the best for everyone, including David."

"No. This is about you. Your reputation, your goddamn pride. Say your plan works. Say you get lucky and find him in time, or the antimatter doesn't kill them. How do you think David will feel, knowing you risked his life just so you could get in the Network's good graces again?"

Rynyan stared down at the prism in his hands, breathing hard. "But… My motives are good, Nashira. I gain status by helping others. It's symbiotic!"

She shook her head. "You were so close. I almost thought you'd figured it out."

"What?"

"That it's easy to be charitable when it doesn't cost you anything. The real test is when you really have to give something up. What about you and me? You gave up hitting on me because you understood that it wasn't what I wanted. Didn't you?"

"Yes, but… as deeply as I regret losing that opportunity, there are many other females just as enticing. This… this is a unique opportunity. And not just for me!"

"Exactly. This is one time you have to make a real choice, Rynyan. One where you lose something either way, just like the rest of us. So you have to decide. Do you want to save your reputation with total strangers, with those jerks back home you don't even like? Or do you want David to trust you again?"

Rynyan thought it over for a long while. Finally, he looked at her. "I heard your offer to Tsshar. Keeping the list secret would benefit you as well. But... you're not asking for your sake. Only for David's."

Nashira flushed. She hadn't realized that herself. "I guess... the kid's a bad influence."

Rynyan answered very softly. "Maybe we can learn something from humans after all." After a bit more hesitation, he handed her the prism. "I'll keep your secret. Just... get our David back."

5

The Hub vector that Tsshar Murieff's crew "discovered" on one of its salvaged artifacts turned out to open just a few astronomical units from the archive's current position. The rescue ship needed less than a day to reach the structure, locate a docking port, and retrieve David, Julio, and Jojjimok. Its personnel then attached thruster pods to the archive to nudge it off the newer Hubpoint so that the ship could return through it, saving time and fuel. Perhaps the archive would eventually be moved back around one of the two Hubpoints for the benefit of the archaeologists who would no doubt make their careers studying its contents.

But that mattered little to Nashira, for she'd scored several gains of her own. The vector list was still a secret she shared with Tsshar's crew, potentially her ticket out of the scouting life. David was safe—which mattered more to her than she would have realized before today. And even Rynyan might have finally begun to look beyond his bubble of entitlement and become less of a nuisance. The Sosyryn seemed genuinely humbled by recent events as he stood by Nashira's side to greet David upon his exit from the rescue ship, as a gaggle of reporters and news drones hovered nearby (figuratively and literally, in that order).

Still, Nashira kept her cool as David approached. "I told you, kid. This is what happens when you go haring off after strange aliens. Next time, you might not be so lucky."

"Oh, I don't know," David said. "It turned out pretty well. I got to go someplace amazing, and I made some new friends." He patted the arms of the burly human and blubbery Hijjeg who flanked him.

"Yes, yes," said Tsshar as she hopped up onto David's shoulders. "We show you a good time. And you come home safe, thanks to Manager Zynara here."

David's eyes widened. "Really?" Rynyan visibly resisted the urge to preen.

"Yes, tell us, Rynyan," called out a Heurhot reporter amid the gaggle, "how did you ever manage to claim *two* new Hubpoints in one day? And what museums and institutions do you plan on donating your finds to?"

"What?" Rynyan cried. "No, no, *I* didn't claim the Hubpoints."

"Don't be modest, Rynyan. We've confirmed the filing in Hubstation records." Her drone belched a cloud of nanofog into the air, projecting a text readout onto it to confirm her assertion.

David's face fell. "I should've known, Rynyan. You just couldn't resist putting yourself first again."

"No! Tsshar was supposed to claim the archive! David, you don't know what I passed up! I—" He stopped short of mentioning the vector list, aware of the many cameras upon him. He was forced to stand and watch mutely as a disappointed David moved off to talk with his fellow rescuees. Then the journalistic blob swallowed him up and he was lost to view.

Nashira moved to confront Tsshar. "You filed the claims in Rynyan's name, didn't you?"

The striped Mrwadj looked up with limpid-eyed innocence. "I can be charitable too, if I want."

"Bullshit. You just wanted to avoid being linked with the archive. It's too public now for the likes of you."

Tsshar hopped onto her shoulders and whispered in her ear. "For the likes of *us*. Let Rynyan have his little archive; we have the vector list. We find plenty more wealth. Whole worlds full."

The reminder was enough to ease Nashira's qualms. Still, for the first time, she actually felt bad for Rynyan. Maybe she should tell David what had really happened.

So when Tsshar scampered back toward her crew, Nashira followed. When she caught up, she found the brown-furred captain staring in surprise at David, who stood there holding Art, a Fishy Intelligence, in his cylindrical tank. "You find my fish!" Tsshar cried. "And I hide it so well!"

"He's my fish, Tsshar," David reminded her gently.

Art blurbled and blinked up at him. "Biometrics accepted. Primary user."

"He is now," Tsshar granted. "You earn him. And you pass the audition. Welcome to my crew!"

"Crew?" David was startled. "I don't know, Tsshar. You guys... the things you do..."

The big engineer, Julio Rodriguez, laughed and clapped him on the shoulder. "Is it any more disreputable than quantelope cold-calling? A job you've probably lost now anyway, what with missing several days of work. And believe me, this job pays a lot better. I could even help you with your Hub studies, if you like."

David looked to Nashira. "What do you think? Is this a good idea?"

She moved in closer. "Well... I've made my own little arrangement with Tsshar. So I'll be around to keep an eye on you." She shrugged. "It's okay with me."

He smiled. "Wow. All right, then—I guess I'm a space pirate now!"

"Thief, not pirate," Tsshar said. "Pirates use force. We use wits, finesse."

"Oh, like how your crew grabbed me and ripped off all my stuff when I came aboard?"

"Self-defense! Brought it on yourself. You learn better. Plenty more to learn. After you rest." She wrinkled her nose. "And bathe. Especially bathe." She scampered off.

Nashira gave David a sidelong look. "Hold on. How'd you manage to find your fish thing?"

David fidgeted. "I didn't." He glanced over to Julio. "Thanks for finding it for me. But... why? The test was to see if I was a good enough thief. But I'd never have found Art without your help. So what can I really contribute to this crew?"

The big, bare-chested man smiled at him and stroked the side of his face. "Maybe I was just thinking of what you could contribute to me." He then pulled David into a warm embrace and a very serious kiss... which David eagerly returned a moment later.

Nashira gaped at the sight. Normally she would have quite enjoyed it, but in this case...

"Oh, my." Rynyan must have extricated himself from the reporter horde, for he stood beside her now, looking impressed as the kiss went on. "Our David certainly has a way of endearing himself to people he gets stranded with. First you, now this strapping fellow."

Nashira glared at him, flushing. "What's that supposed to mean?"

"Come now, my dear. I may have misconstrued your interest in me, but a little objectivity does wonders." He affected a broad wink.

"I don't know what you're talking about."

"Such an interesting phrase. Humans only seem to use it when they know exactly what you're talking about."

She sighed. "Okay, maybe. But it's obviously one-sided."

"Oh, David's just too shy to express his attraction."

Julio picked David up in his arms and carried him off, saying something about getting him that bath the captain had ordered.

Rynyan blinked. "At least, he was."

"Well, he's made his choice. If I had a chance, I didn't take it, and that's on me."

Rynyan nodded in understanding. "Sometimes being a good friend means not getting what you want."

She studied him. Maybe he sincerely was starting to learn. And he had kept the vector list secret—mainly for David's benefit, but perhaps for hers as well. She owed him gratitude for that, however grudging.

"So did you sort things out with the press?" she asked as they made their way back to the Hubstation concourse.

He sighed. "No. They're still convinced I'm the one who rescued the crew and revealed the archive to the Network. I'm a hero again," he finished dejectedly.

"Look... David's fair. He'll forgive you eventually. Maybe if you just... keep trying to earn it."

"I agree. That's why I intend to keep the station manager job—to earn my penance, if you will. Learn some real humility."

"You really think you can pull it off? You're four hundred years old and you've never worked a day."

Rynyan preened his mane haughtily. "I may still be young, but I'll have you know that managing hundreds of charity operations at once is quite an involved process. There have been times when I've had to spend as much as three hours a day giving instructions to my staff."

"How awful for you." They both had to raise their voices over the clamor of the concourse now.

"I understand I'll have to be much more 'in the trenches' in this job, but I'm certain I can adapt. I just need a comfortable grace period, and I'm sure I can ease into—"

Passing through the arch into the main concourse, they saw a frenzied crowd seething around the manager's office, screaming about delayed flights, lost luggage, overdue maintenance, hotel room misallocations, and a dozen other things Nashira's translator couldn't parse. Rynyan ducked behind Nashira's back, but not before the mob spotted his shimmering mane and began to surge toward them.

"Nashira?"

"Yes?"

"I need your assistance."

COUNT TWO

...AND HE BUILT A CROOKED HUB

(With apologies to Robert A. Heinlein and the Marx Brothers)

6

"So. You and Julio, huh?"

Nashira Wing had run into David LaMacchia outside the offices of Hubstation 3742's ship maintenance section. She was there to oversee the removal of some of Rynyan's well-intentioned "upgrades" to the *Starship Entropy*—really, she was fine with the more efficient engines, the higher-resolution display wall, and the comfier pilot's seat, but she did *not* need a hot tub in place of her emergency rations locker—while David was tagging along with *Miifu*'s crew as they worked on reconfiguring the ship's secret compartments in the wake of its recent search by Hubstation security. Tsshar and Julio were in a meeting with the maintenance chief, making sure all the specifications and bribes were in order, and David and Nashira watched them through the office window.

"Whoof," Nashira went on, admiring Julio's muscular bum. "You are one lucky bastard. He's gorgeous."

David smiled. "Yes, he is. And kind and smart and funny... I've never been so happy."

Nashira forced down a twinge of jealousy, though she wasn't sure which man she was more jealous of. She distracted herself by focusing on shallower matters. "And a wizard in the sack, right?"

Her young friend blushed. "I, um... I don't think a gentleman should kiss and tell."

"You can skip the snogging bits—just get right to the good stuff. Come on, I want graphic sexual details! That's what friends do, right? They share *everything*."

David laughed uneasily. "Well... honestly, I'm not even sure how to put it into words. I'm not that… experienced."

"With men?"

"With anyone. Julio's only the third person I've ever gone all the way with. The second man."

Nashira stared. "Fair dinkum? You're the one who's bi, and I've rooted more women than you have. That's sad."

"Well, my luck's improved in a big way now," David said. His eyes widened as if an idea had occurred to him. "Just like your luck's bound to change now that you've got that vector list, right?"

It was an unsubtle attempt to change the subject, but Nashira took mercy on him—for now. "Sure, if I ever get the *Entropy* back on the line. I mean, the wait helps in a way—it lets me tack vectors from the list onto my assigned slate as overtime dives to make up for the lost time. Keeps them from looking suspicious. But I hate waiting when I know the find of a lifetime could be just days away."

David caressed her back, and her breath caught. "I just know you'll find something that's worth the wait. Something that'll benefit the whole Hub Network and put humanity on the map at last. I hoped I'd be the one to do that, but I'll be just as happy if it's you, my friend."

Nashira pulled away before he could draw her into a hug. She was dealing with enough frustration without that. She made some excuse to leave the office, then headed for the nearest bar. She needed some casual, random sex as a distraction. It was deeply unfair that shy, awkward David was getting more and better cock than she was—and wouldn't even share the juicy details.

"Yes, the Skahgahfah are the most extraordinary animals," one Jiikdik was saying to another as the purple-shelled arthropods preceded David into the receiving area of the Tpohspafh Auction House. It spread its forward two pairs of limbs and went on, "Second-largest known animals in the greater galaxy. Bigger than a six-family hive, nine limbs, two heads, prismatic plumage, able to produce the most beautiful harmonies. When a full herd was in mating season, you could hear their soul-wrenching melodies across half the continent."

"And now there are only a few dozen left," the other Jiikdik said, smacking its mandibles. "I can't wait to kill one!"

"You think I'd let you settle for just one? Our hunting craft is equipped with every amenity for the dedicated sportsbeing seeking to pit one's wits and courage against brutish nature: over a dozen high-yield missiles, plasma rays that could burn through a mountain, poison gas that kills in seconds, defoliants that raze whole forests so the prey has nowhere to hide. All controlled by thought commands from a luxurious control couch with all the amenities—you won't even have to lift a pincer!"

David was relieved when the hunters drifted out of his earshot. Still, their nauseating conversation made him feel better about his part in ripping these people off. His qualms of conscience about turning to a life of crime were eased by the fact that Captain Murieff and the crew of *Miifu* mainly targeted the wealthiest Hub Network citizens—not out of any Robin Hood ethic, but merely because they had the most to steal. While the Sosyryn prided themselves—to a fault—on giving away their endless wealth, there were others in the Network driven to accumulate and hoard as much wealth as possible, and to show off their conspicuous consumption to their peers. Some of them took it to obnoxious excess, such as the people who had bought the entire planet Tpohspafh—whose pre-sapient life was going through a phase of gigantism that made Earth's dinosaurs seem unambitious—and paid the most expensive lawyers in the Network to find and exploit every possible loophole in the environmental protection laws, allowing them to turn the planet into a hunting preserve where the idle rich of the greater galaxy could indulge their fetish for heavy weapons banned almost everywhere else in the Network.

David had no chance of halting the barbaric practice, but at least he could help screw up the auction that the planet's rich visitors were holding here—a chance for them to show off and trade their most extravagant art and artifacts, many plundered from ancient ruins or acquired through illicit deals. A few items from the now-famous pre-Network archive, from some of the first lots plundered and sold by Tsshar before she had stolen

David, had already made their way here, though *Miifu*'s crew was not here to steal them back—yet. According to Julio, they were here for a museum heist—which made David wonder what they were doing at an auction house instead.

Sweat was forming under the brim of the delivery worker's cap David wore, but he couldn't risk fumbling the crate he carried in order to wipe his brow—not if he wanted to stay in the captain's good graces. His eyes were stinging by the time he got to the check-in desk and plopped the crate down atop it. "A new lot for the auction," he told the cadaverous Jiodeyn cashier. "From the Hwaieur estate. Last-minute thing. They've got a lot of legal fees to cover after the Zeghryk thing, y'know."

The cashier studied the crate with her four small black eyes. "Are those air holes? Is there something moving in there?"

The crate's lid sprang open and a brown, striped furball leapt into the cashier's arms. "Hello!" Tsshar Murieff effused. "I am putting myself in a box for you!"

"Mrwadj!" the cashier cried. "Call secu-mmph!" Tsshar clambered over her elongated face.

David took the opportunity to sneak away from the desk while his captain flowed sinuously across the cashier's quadruple shoulders. "Do not worry," she told the Jiodeyn, dodging the arms trying to pull her off. "I am only making a distraction, because I am irresistible. See how hard you try to hug me? Ooh, what's in your pockets?" she asked, her deft, long digits rifling through the cashier's uniform in a blur of brown. "Vault keys? Deposit box keys? House keys? I like keys!"

Security had finally taken notice, but the guards ran right by David as he sauntered toward the exit with feigned casualness. For once, he was grateful that humans were invisible in the Network.

Once he was outside, though, Julio ran past at top speed, grabbing David's hand and pulling his lover after him. "I've got it! Let's go!"

"Got what?" David gasped as they ran.

Julio pulled open one side of his vest to give David a glimpse of an ornate box poking out of its inner pocket, bouncing against his beautifully muscled, sweat-sheened bare chest as he ran.

David admired both aspects of the view, but was confused. "Is that going to help us with the museum heist?"

"This *was* the museum heist! Now, move your ass! I want to be long gone before they figure out I swapped it for a fake."

Although "long gone" proved to be a relative term, since getting back to *Miifu* required sneaking aboard the space elevator for a six-hour ride back to the orbital dock. Once Julio broke into the elevator carriage's cargo compartment and led David to a safe, secluded corner, the two sweaty, adrenaline-drunk lovers laughed long and hard, then fell into a passionate embrace and tore at each other's clothes. Six hours hardly seemed long enough.

Still, they had some time afterward to snuggle and talk. "This is so much more fun now that I can share it with you," Julio said.

"It is exciting," David replied. "I wish I could do more than just carry boxes and be a lookout, though."

"You will in time. You're still learning the craft. For now, just trust in me. I'll take care of you."

"Then are you ever going to tell me what we stole? And where this museum is that you stole it from?"

Julio laughed and rummaged through his discarded clothes until he found and retrieved the ornate box. "The Fioathob Gallery," he intoned. "The final legacy of an extinct nanite civilization, hoarded for centuries by private collectors. There are thousands of precious, microscopic works of art and historical artifacts inside—held in place by superstrong magnetic fields, so there was no need to be gentle." He tossed it over.

David caught it clumsily and stared in amazement. If he looked closely enough, the patterns in the side of the box did appear to contain very tiny windows. "So when you said 'museum heist'…"

"I meant it literally." Julio struck a dashing pose. "A lesser boyfriend would merely take you to the museum. I bring the museum to you."

"I appreciate the thought," David said, turning the museum in his hands in search of an entrance. "But it's like I told you before about fine art—I don't think I can really get into it."

When Nashira emerged from the short corridor between the *Starship Entropy* and the Scout Center's staging area, Rynyan spotted her through the central office's window and hopped up from his desk, his long legs carrying him swiftly out of the office to meet her midway. "Welcome back, Nashira! Did you have a good day's scouting?" He gave her a pronounced, unsubtle wink. "Find anything valuable?"

She sighed. "Not yet. Had another close call, though—the telescope detected the ruins of an ancient megastructure three parsecs from the Hubpoint. I took the usual scans—hopefully it'll give the scientists something worthwhile to chew on."

"I don't doubt it. You're getting closer! The last one was four parsecs away. It's only a matter of time, my dear."

"It's been over two weeks. I thought I'd find something by now."

"You must simply be patient. Why, look at Mansura!"

Nashira stared. "What about her?"

"Come, see for yourself. They're giving her a sendoff in the ready room."

They found Mansura Joumari in the midst of an awkwardly festive gathering of scouts, including Evdrae, Stauats, and a few others. Nashira recognized the mood from the few times she'd seen it happen to other scouts. "You're getting out?" she asked the mature Moroccan, barely able to mask the envy in her voice.

Mansura smiled. "My discovery bonus just cleared. A new Hubpoint only two light-months from a red dwarf system. With two planets showing spectral signatures of liquid water and microbial photosynthesis."

"Oh, very well recited, Mansura!" Stauats loomed over the two women and patted Mansura on the head with his furry, prehensile proboscis. The lanky, purple-brown Flanx turned to Nashira and spoke in a slow, loud voice. "She finds good star! Star with life! No people, not close to go to, but still good for learning!"

Nashira rolled her eyes. "Yes, I get it, Dongerface. I've only been doing this job for—" She broke off, knowing how futile it was to convince Stauats of the obvious.

Although there was a part she didn't get. Leading the older woman over to the snack table, she said, "Good onya, Mansura. That's a nice big bonus... but not exactly the gold ring, you know?" A find like this would have long-term benefits to scientists, but would not benefit the Network as much as a Hubpoint within travel range of a new civilization or habitable planet. The bonus for the discoverer was commensurately less.

Mansura smiled. "Nashira, I've spent the past seven years working toward this. Living on a budget, investing my income responsibly. With this bonus, I'm finally over the top, and then some. I'm debt-free and have enough saved up to relocate to the next ring inward, start a shipping business with some contacts I've cultivated there."

"No worry, Nashira!" Stauats stiltedly Flanx-splained. "She leaves this place, but still lives! There are other places like this! Not your people's so-called 'afterlife,' but better than this!" Nashira shoved a bowl of dip into his proboscis to shut him up.

"You could learn from your elders, Nashira," said Evdrae, a yellow-skinned Druagom female with a bright orange head crest and throat sac. "Maybe you wouldn't be so deep in debt if you didn't squander your earnings on parties, intoxicants, and males."

Nashira glared at the snide amphibian. "I only drink to forget."

"Forget what?"

"Conversations like this one. And by the way? I guarantee I'll earn out before you do."

"Only if I dive into a star before you do."

"There you go trying to cheer me up again."

Mansura put a hand on Nashira's shoulder. "I admire your confidence, but in her own way, Evdrae has a point. I've told you many times, you'd be much closer to this if you lived more frugally."

"If I'd tried living that way, I'd have jumped out an airlock within a year." It was a familiar, practiced response, but it stuck in her throat when she realized it was the last time she'd have this argument with Mansura. She was glad the older woman had gotten out of the life this way instead of the more sudden and violent way that most Hub scouts' careers ended, but the Scout Center would be a harsher, more cutthroat place without her calming influence.

"Don't worry," Rynyan told her later, when she expressed some of this. "You'll probably be following her out within weeks. It's only fair, considering that it's thanks to you she got out."

"What do you mean?"

"Oh, she volunteered for extra dives last week. And since I've been sneaking vectors from the archive list into your dive schedule, I had a fair number of leftover vectors waiting to be assigned, so I gave them to her."

Nashira managed to hold in her scream of frustration until she reached the showers. That find should've been hers! True, it wouldn't have benefited her as much as it had Mansura. And she hoped for more than the opportunity to migrate inward to a more upscale ring of the Hubcomplex; she dreamed of a prize that would free her to go anywhere in nine galaxies and spend the rest of her life in luxury. Still, a find like that would've been a major step forward in clearing her debts. She'd lost a sure thing in order to gamble on something much bigger.

She tried to relax under the hot shower, but the tension in her muscles had barely begun to ease when her water ration ran out and the forceful blasts of the air dryer kicked in. Someone had set the air stream to high heat, and she leapt out of the shower tube half-scalded and still dripping. "That damn list had *better* pay off soon," she muttered through clenched teeth. She was starting to think it would've been easier to join Tsshar's crew and become a thief, like David.

"We should do more than rob this place," David said to Julio as they emerged from the rear exit of the L'myekist monastery, carrying a crate full of the tithes and treasures the missionaries of L'myek had persuaded their converts to renounce into their care. Above them, the ornately carved and buttressed, gold- and gemstone-adorned walls of the monastery glistened in the light of the planet M'visakul's two moons, outshining even the natural crystal formations of the Jeweled Mountain atop which it perched. "We should expose the L'myekists' scam to the whole greater galaxy. If people saw that *this* was what they did with the possessions all their converts have to renounce—"

Tsshar hopped on top of the crate, making David stumble. "People know," she told him. "Those who want to know, know. People who don't want to know—they don't know."

"Look at all the rich, opulent churches on Earth," Julio said. "Preachers worshipping greed and building palaces to themselves, yet people still think they stand for selfless giving and spirituality."

"Churches are the best thieves," Tsshar said with admiration. "Make people want to be stolen from, and think it's a gift to them." She cuffed David's head with a paw. "And we don't rob the place. Rob means use force or threat. We burgle."

"Okay, we should do more than burgle the place. The older worlds may know what they do, but what about people back on Earth, and other new members? Somebody should get the word out."

"We get the loot out. That's better." She hopped onto David's shoulders, clinging to his back. "It's good to make suggestions, little David. I want you useful for more than carrying things. But make good suggestions. Suggest things to steal. Suggest ways to steal, or ways to hide. Exposing isn't hiding. Find better ways to help—or I find bigger someone to carry things."

She leapt off his back and scampered toward the ship. He staggered and fell face-down in the dirt road, dropping his side of the crate, which cracked open and spilled dozens of pieces of antique metalware all around him. Julio set his end of the crate down and helped David up. "Are you all right?"

"I've had worse," David said. He looked around at the mess and sighed. "Tsshar's right. I'm next to useless to you guys."

"Don't take it so hard," Julio said, crouching down to pick up the fallen antiques. "She's just trying to motivate you. We all want you to succeed."

David joined him in the cleanup. "Well, I hope I get the hang of this soon," he replied. He was starting to wish he had some secret weapon to give him a surefire path to success, like Nashira.

7

Nashira cursed as a trio of pyramid-shaped alien drones released a swarm of missiles at her Hubdiver craft. She fired the *Starship Entropy*'s thrusters, fully aware that they lacked the power for this kind of evasive maneuvering.

"Stand down! Noncombatant! I come in peace! I bloody surrender!" she screamed into the comm pickup, hoping the drones could somehow interpret her language, even though their own warnings had been broadcast in a tongue too ancient to be recorded in the Hub Network's databases. In between her desperate shouts, she wished she'd never found that damned address list. It should've been her golden ticket, a treasure map leading to unparalleled discoveries. Instead, it had led her to this.

Nashira scanned the sky for the scintillant speck of laser light marking the Hubpoint, her one hope of escape from the oncoming missiles. But the four-minute grace period had ended, the Hubpoint was closed, and she didn't have time to signal for its reopening. She barely even had time to scream a curse as the first missile closed to impact—

—and bounced harmlessly off the *Entropy*'s hull.

"The rest of the missiles either missed or fizzled out in their launch tubes," Nashira reported later, as she stood in the repair bay back at Hubstation 3742. "The ones that detonated had about as much kick as American beer."

Next to her, Rynyan Zynara ad Surynyyyyyy'a examined the minor damage to the *Entropy*, folding his tapering fingers across his chest. "Well, they were two hundred thousand years old," he said. "Really, it's a testament to their builders' skill that the drones even operated."

"I'm glad you're so impressed by the things that almost killed me."

"Oh, Nashira, you know I have the utmost confidence in your abilities."

Nashira still wasn't used to having a manager who actually liked her. She hardly returned the sentiment; the hyper-wealthy, self-entitled Sosyryn had been a nuisance to her for years, and she was not yet convinced that his recent good behavior was more than a temporary whim. Still, she wasn't above taking advantage of the opportunity. "Then you'll let me go back?"

Rynyan's leonine features took on a shocked look, his feathery mane puffing outward. "Are you joking? You know I have to put that vector on the dormant list."

"But the drones are duds! Rynyan, there's a habitable planet right there, in easy range of the Hubpoint."

"A planet defended by technologies robust enough to survive two hundred millennia. What are the odds that you just happened to encounter the *last* active defense systems?"

"But this is my best result yet from the vector list! The first planet that's still habitable and hasn't drifted too far from its Hubpoint."

Nashira had thought the ancient list would be a Hub scout's ultimate cheat sheet, a quick and easy way out of this mind-numbing career. But getting frustratingly close to a major find this routinely—using the Hub to travel instantaneously across thousands of parsecs, yet having no way to cover the remaining few light-years or even light-months to claim the prize—was turning out to be even worse than "discovering" random bits of empty intergalactic space thirty times a day.

"Rynyan, you've got to give me another shot," she pleaded. "Send a military escort with me, let them deal with the drones."

"You know the rules, Nashira. I simply can't. Not without solid evidence that there's something there worth the risk."

"It's worth it to me! You can't get it. You Sosyryn have so many riches you can't give them away fast enough. You can't know what it's like not to get what you want."

"You have given me an education in that, my dear," he told her with a rueful smile.

"And how many other hetero females have ever said no to you?"

He preened. "Virtually none. Never as persistently as you, anyway. I admire your conviction, even if your taste bewilders me."

"Then, no, Rynyan, you don't get it at all. *Once* in nine years of diving, I found something that could've been my ticket, and *someone* stole it out from under me."

He fidgeted under her accusing glare. "Well, if it's any consolation, Rynyan's Rings has become a very popular holiday spot."

"It isn't," she told him through clenched teeth.

"Look... I could simply give you the bonus, as a favor for my dear friend. You need only ask."

She stiffened. "I won't take charity, Rynyan. Giving me leeway to earn it is one thing, but I won't be dependent on anyone, least of all you."

He cocked his head in puzzlement. "Even though I'm no longer trying to... what's the phrase... get into your plant?"

Despite herself, she laughed. "One, whose grandmum did you hear that from? Two, it's 'pants.' Get into my pants."

"Oh, now you're just toying with me. How could we copulate if I were wearing your pants? Besides, the plant metaphor makes sense, especially if it's a flower such as a—"

Nashira had never been more grateful to be pounced on by a Mrwadj. A child-sized mass of tiger-striped brown-orange fur and spider-monkey limbs landed atop her head and shoulders, sending her staggering as a dewy-eyed, kittenish face with whiskery feeding tendrils lowered itself into her line of sight. "Hello, little Nashira human!" Tsshar Murieff mewled. "*Miifu* is back, with much successes to celebrate!"

Speak of the devil, Nashira thought as she regained her balance and her breath. She should have gotten used to the Mrwadj captain's disregard for personal space by now. Then again, maybe she had; she managed to get a good grip on Tsshar before the little thief could dodge. Once she set the small alien down, a quick pat-down of Tsshar's garment turned up personal items pilfered from two of Nashira's jumpsuit pockets. "Hey!"

"Good frisking, little Nashira! Get almost all of it!"

"Almost?!"

"Yes!" Tsshar hopped away, brandishing Nashira's credit rod. "Come, join my crew and boast of profitable scouting!"

Nashira's hand smacked her pocket, feeling the rod's absence. "Oh, for—We'll continue this later, Rynyan!" she yelled as she ran after the larcenous little cat-monkey. She had no patience for Tsshar's thieving ways, for they were largely responsible for Nashira's current situation.

The laughter and jovial chatter Nashira heard as she neared *Miifu*'s docking bay merely threw her dark mood into sharper relief. Clearly Tsshar's crew of thieves and scoundrels had profited well on their latest venture. Nashira could only hope the Mrwadj captain would not blame her for failing to somehow intuit the most viable vectors, take back the list, and hire some other scout to be her front.

Nashira shook off her anxiety and strode into the docking bay. If nothing else, David would be there. His company was the one thing that Nashira could always count on to cheer her up—though heaven forbid she should ever admit it to his face.

That face, as it turned out, was currently locked in a passionate kiss with Julio Rodriguez. Nashira felt a twinge of frustration that the burly, dreadlocked engineer and science officer had snatched David up before she'd consciously admitted that she wanted him for herself—but she had to admit, it was quite pleasant to watch the two men going at it. David was reasonably appealing in a cornfed sort of way, but Julio was a knockout and very well aware of it. Nashira was very grateful for his habit of wearing only a sleeveless, open vest on his muscular upper torso.

"About time you catch up!" Tsshar brushed affectionately against Nashira's side. The scout caught the captain's hand a moment later as it slipped out of Nashira's pocket. Once Nashira wrenched her credit rod and crystal drive free from Tsshar's long, fine fingers, the Mrwadj jumped clear, then brandished the human's watch in triumph. Nashira kept forgetting that

Tsshar had twice as many hands as she did.

"Get faster!" Tsshar urged as she dodged Nashira's lunge. "Aim better! We make you a good thief, like little David!"

Nashira's eyes widened. "David? *LaMacchia?*"

"Yes! Little human tells us of the Ziovris. How they reverse their migration to the far Hubpoint when he finds a second Hubpoint closer by."

"When *he* finds it? That was—" Nashira quashed her protest, not wanting to undermine David in the eyes of his crew. Besides, it hadn't really been her discovery either, as proven by the continued near-emptiness of her credit rod.

"That's right," Julio said, belatedly noticing Nashira. "Altering the momentum of such a massive migration is bound to result in some disruption, Ziovris efficiency notwithstanding. Valuable goods and cultural artifacts meant for one destination being hastily rerouted to another..." He shrugged. "Well, things are bound to be misplaced."

"And if we volunteer to carry some extra cargo," Tsshar added, "we can 'misplace' some of it into our place. Clerical error. So sad. But a small glitch in the huge plan."

"That's genuinely clever," Nashira had to admit. "And *David* thought of it?"

"That's right," Julio beamed, ignoring her incredulous tone as he stroked David's shoulder. "He's becoming quite an effective scoundrel."

"Oh, I can't take the credit for it," David demurred.

"Sure you can," Julio replied through clenched teeth.

"No, I just told Julio about our experiences with the Ziovris. Siphoning off from the migration was his idea."

Tsshar stared between them. "It's your idea, Julio?"

"David, you're being too modest," Julio insisted.

"No, this was your victory. You deserve the credit."

"I see," Tsshar said, sounding disappointed—in part because Nashira had taken advantage of the Mrwadj's distraction to steal back her watch.

"Then, Julio, you are still a fine scoundrel," Tsshar went on. "You can come, help secure the best prizes *you* win for us. Other humans stay here. Come, come, little one." She tugged at the much bigger man's hand until he gave in and headed off after her, throwing a fond but frustrated look at David.

Nashira gave the young man a similar look. "You're an idiot, you know that? Julio just wants you to have Tsshar's respect so she'll keep you around."

David smiled. "I know, Nashira. But I learned the hard way about taking charity. I don't want any privileges in this crew that I don't earn for myself."

She admired his conviction, but that very honesty was ill-suited for success among this crew of thieves and vagabonds. "Julio means well, but he's trying to draw you deeper into a world where you just don't belong. You're not meant to be a criminal, kid."

"We don't hurt anybody. We take stuff, but more stuff is easy to get in the Network. I'm just learning to adapt to an alien culture." He clasped her shoulders. "And don't worry. I trust Julio to look out for me."

He headed off to find his lover, leaving Nashira alone with her frustration. She'd been protecting David from himself since his first week at the Hubcomplex. But how could she keep protecting him if he no longer felt he needed her? Once again, her goal was just beyond her grasp.

"I appreciate what you tried to do," David said to Julio that evening as he tapped the code for Room 4 into Suite 47's entry pad. "But you really shouldn't have."

Before *Miifu*'s engineer could answer, the door slid open, unleashing a noisome smell and a suite of slavering, tearing, bone-crunching sounds. "David, it's Opmlqh!" came a muffled voice from within. "You got Room 5 again. Don't worry, I'm just finishing up dinner! The rest of him is safely in the hospital by now. But you and your delectable friend are welcome to join me for dessert! Or better yet, *as* dessert!"

David echoed her laughter. "Thanks, Millie, but you know human limbs don't grow back!"

"Medical science *can* do wonders, you know. And you won't feel a thing once my venom kicks in."

"A flattering offer, madam," Julio purred in his best

sexy-pirate voice. "I shall give it serious thought for later."

The huge, slavering Qhpong tittered. "Oh, you're an inveterate flirt!"

The tesseract suite's dimensional interface connected properly to Room 4 on the second try, and David led his boyfriend inside. "I mean it, Julio. You've got to stop giving me credit for your ideas. I want to earn my own way."

Julio sighed as he let his rucksack fall onto the tattered couch. "David, in a whole month, you haven't successfully stolen one thing without my help. You're too damn honest. You'll never earn Tsshar's respect if we can't convince her you're devious enough to be a thief."

"I know, I know. Ownership has to be earned. I respect her values, really, and I'm trying to adapt. But I never will if you keep coddling me."

The bigger man stroked his arm. "I'm just trying to nudge you in the wrong direction."

"You're giving me charity. I took charity from Rynyan, but it turned out he was just being selfish." David would've forgiven Rynyan if he had been the only one hurt by the Sosyryn's carelessness. But in his eagerness to out-donate his fellow Sosyryn, Rynyan had recklessly partnered with Hwaieur Aytriaew's fanatical group, who had used his charity efforts as a cover for an attack on an entire world—and who would have targeted Earth next if Nashira hadn't exposed them. David wasn't a vindictive person, but that was a hard thing to get over.

Julio pulled him closer. "Well, I'm being selfish too. I really, really want to keep you around." He underlined his point with a passionate kiss.

Once he was let up for air, David replied, "Which is why we can't keep going on like this. Eventually Tsshar's going to realize you're carrying me, and then we'll both be off this crew." He stroked Julio's dreadlocks and kissed him back. "I don't want to be responsible for that. So you have to let me succeed or fail on my own."

"But—"

"No. I'm putting my foot down. No more stealing things or coming up with plans in my name. Got it?"

Julio sighed. "Got it."

"Good." David kissed him some more.

"Except—"

David stared. "Julio, what did you do?"

The muscular engineer stepped over to his rucksack and brought out a metallic box about forty centimeters on a side. It seemed like a distorted cube at first, but David soon realized its faces were diamond-shaped and more numerous than a cube's. "It's an octacube safe," Julio said. "The latest in high-end dimensional security. Same principle as this suite, but it's got twenty-four interior cells instead of eight—plus added security features. See?" He unfolded a couple of the angular faces, revealing an empty interior. "Here—give me your shirt."

David pulled off his shirt and handed it to Julio. "Why? You never wear one."

"Because we won't miss it." Grinning, Julio tossed the shirt inside, closed the safe, and reopened it. The interior was empty again.

"Hey!" David took the ocatacube, closed it, reopened it—still nothing. "What gives?"

"Like I said, twenty-four hyperdimensional compartments. Things go in, but they don't come out—not unless you know the combination to align the interface with one of the occupied cells. Tsshar keeps some of her most precious valuables in this. Hell, the safe itself is rare and precious."

David stared. "And you stole it? And brought it here?"

Julio grinned. "That's right. And it no doubt has a tracking device built in, so it'll lead Tsshar right to this room. All you have to do is take credit."

"Oh, Julio, she'll never believe it. You were the last one she took to her storeroom."

"She'll believe it if you can crack the combination. I just stole it to give you a chance." Julio handed it to him. "Come on. You want to prove yourself? Take everything Tsshar and I have taught you. Use every resource at your disposal. Crack the safe."

David stared at the octacube for a long time. "I... have no idea what to do."

A sigh. "David! You gave me that big speech—"

"Wait! I have it! Art!"

Julio groaned. "Not your stupid fish!"

David carried the safe over to the bedside table, setting it next to the cylindrical tank in which the bizarre, globular bioengineered creature swam idly. The tank's base now bore a handprinted label reading ART, A FISHY INTELLIGENCE.

"Not a fish. A biocomputer. He's been helping me with my Hub studies—maybe he can help with this."

"And exactly how helpful has he been so far?"

Ignoring him, David tapped Art's bowl. "Hey, Art! Got a job for you."

The blobby piscid blinked its upper eye at him. "Primary user identified."

"Take a look at this, Art. It's an octacube safe. Do you know about those?"

Art burbled loudly for a moment. "Hyperdimensional security containment device, Mark H-41. Exploits hyperspatial topology of Hub-adjacent spacetime to generate a twenty-four-cell uniform polychoron configuration with pseudo-randomized three-space projection to preclude unauthorized removal of contents."

"Great. Do you know how to crack its combination?"

Julio sighed. "How can you figure it out on your own if you ask your fish from Hell to do it for you?"

"You said to use my resources. Art's my resource."

The biocomputer finished mulling over the question. "Security override procedures not publicly available. Analysis of interior mechanism may allow calculation of override method."

"You could do that?"

"The sensoria within this biocomputer and its containment unit are potentially capable of the task, given access to interior mechanism."

"Great!" Opening the top flaps, David picked up Art's bowl and began lowering him inside.

"Um, David?" Julio asked.

David removed his empty hands from the safe. "Now go to work, Art! Good boy!"

"David—"

The opened flaps closed automatically.

David turned to Julio. "The flaps close automatically, don't they?" Julio nodded.

They both leapt for the box and pulled open the flaps. Art was nowhere to be seen. "Art!" David called. "Can you hear me, little guy?" There was no reply.

"If he does crack the combination," Julio asked, "can he enter it from inside?"

"Not unless it's a voice combination."

"And unless there's an audio pickup inside."

David peered at the safe appraisingly. "Well... it *might* be big enough for Tsshar to fall into... so she'd want a way to get out..."

They stared for a while, but nothing happened. Finally, they both sat heavily on David's bed. "We need to think of something else," David said.

After a minute of silence, the door slid open. The two shirtless men looked up in surprise to see a gaunt Jiodeyn male staggering into the room, carrying an incongruously massive suitcase in each of his four arms. "Oh, I'm very sorry! I seem to have gotten turned around."

"That's okay," David said. "It happens all the time."

Once the Jiodeyn had staggered out, the two men double-locked the door and resumed pondering. Several minutes later, Julio turned to David. "You know what's good for stimulating the mind?"

"What?"

"Sex." He smiled at David's look. "Seriously. It improves circulation, eases tension, stimulates endorphins. It's great for mental clarity." He pulled David into a passionate embrace.

"Well, okay," David said after a while, pulling at Julio's clothes. "But this is a pretty hard problem to solve."

"Then we'll have to have quite a lot of sex."

"I cannot argue with that logic."

8

After finishing the *Entropy*'s repairs and getting a late, solitary dinner, Nashira headed back to her bunk, eager to let Morpheus's arms smother another frustrating day to its well-deserved death. The route from the Scout Center's repair bay to its pilot dorms took her past the central office, and she was surprised to hear Rynyan's voice emanating from within. Normally, the Sosyryn spent as little time on duty as he could get away with, and he would have been back at his mansion in the elite quarter of Hubstation 9 by now, indulging his relentless fetish for females of different species. She also wasn't accustomed to hearing him sound so nervous and submissive.

Luckily, Sosyryn society was so crime-free and charitable that Rynyan had no concept of door locks, so Nashira was able to slip inside the office to eavesdrop. (On her way in, she mused: *Would Sosyryn burglars break in and* leave *valuables? Bloody hell, Santa Claus would be Public Enemy Number One.*)

Rynyan was in the private quantelope alcove, so Nashira remained unseen. One of the quantum-entangled rodents was speaking in a reedy voice, no doubt a perfect imitation of the speaker at the other end. "You understand why we're concerned about LaMacchia's involvement with the crew that discovered the pre-Network archive," the adorable ansible said. "Given his overt desire to undermine the foundations of Network civilization, the potential… uncontrolled knowledge he might extract creates alarming possibilities."

Rynyan laughed. "Come now, Morjepas, that's quite an exaggeration."

Nashira tensed at the name. Morjepas was the Dosperhag

supervisor in charge of this Hubstation—though he never left Dosp, since his species was too fragile to handle the higher gravity of most populated worlds. Nashira couldn't prove it, but she was convinced that Morjepas was the one who had ordered Rynyan's predecessor to arrange a couple of fatal "accidents" to deter David's Hub research—accidents that would have taken Nashira and Rynyan with him had they succeeded, so she took them rather personally. No one had cracked the secret of predicting Hub vectors in sixteen thousand years, and David was singularly unqualified to break the losing streak; but the Dospers profited immensely from having the Hub within the fringes of their territory, so they feared any research that might threaten their monopoly on interstellar travel. Nashira had managed to make a deal to halt further arranged accidents, but that was when the only threat had been from David's college-dropout education. The ancient archive that Tsshar had plundered came from a far older Hub-centric civilization, possessing knowledge the current Network lacked—including Nashira's vector list. David had stuck with Tsshar's crew partly out of the hope that the plundered artifacts might turn up new secrets of Hub physics. Evidently, David's hope was Morjepas's fear.

To Rynyan's credit, he was making an effort to quell that fear. "David has no interest in undermining anything. He's simply pursuing a personal research project—one whose sheer futility he's too naïve to recognize. It's quite endearing, really."

"I know you found it amusing to fund his investigations," Morjepas replied through the quantelope. "But if you wish to remain in your current position, you must demonstrate your lack of partisanship toward him. Your responsibility is to the entire Network now."

"Of course it is, my friend. And rest assured, I am giving it my all. Though if you don't mind, I am rather late for an assignation with a Bihoqniy collective triad. One mind, three bodies, so many potential combinations."

"You shall have to reschedule. Our agent in LaMacchia's hotel suite is preparing a surveillance report on his activities. You shall remain in your office and relay it to me when it arrives."

Rynyan protested the interference with his vital responsibilities as a galactically renowned lover, but Nashira had other things on her mind. *An agent in David's hotel suite?*

The Hubstation's tesseract suites used a quirk of the physics in the Hub's vicinity to cram a hypercube-shaped assemblage of seven rooms and one entry interface into the volume of a single room. She'd met a number of David's suitemates due to the glitchy interface frequently opening up on the wrong room, but most of its occupants were short-term. Which current tenant was the Dospers' spy? How long had they been there? And what might they be about to report? She struggled to remember if she and David had discussed the vector list in his room. She didn't think they had, but what if he'd talked to Julio about it?

Nashira hurried from the office, determined to warn David—or better yet, to find the spy and intercept their report. She wasn't about to trust Rynyan with her or David's life. Maybe that was unfair, given his recent efforts to redeem himself. But with stakes like these, it was a chance she couldn't take.

Being a trusting sort, David had given Nashira biometric access to his room. So once she reached Suite 47, she punched up Room 4 and barged right in. "David, we need to talk."

She choked out the last word, her mouth drying in the intense burst of freezing air that struck her. Hugging herself—and wishing she hadn't changed into a sleeveless tank top to work on the *Entropy*—she realized that the door control had connected her to the wrong room again, one calibrated for a guest from a methane- or ammonia-based species. The room was vacant save for a large, robotic cleaning cart whose multiple limbs were dumping the old bedsheets into its trash bin and drawing replacements from another receptacle.

"Excuse me," the robot said. "This room is being cleaned and reconfigured for new tenancy. Environmental conditions are in flux. Please depart for your comfort and safety. Should you disregard these instructions and sustain illness or death, all medical or resurrective services shall be charged to your account, and no legal liability shall fall upon Hubstation 3742."

"All right, all right," Nashira got out through chattering

teeth. The reconfiguring explained how she could breathe at all, but she couldn't last long in here. She struggled to get her numb fingers to work the exit control, desperate to retreat to the relative warmth of the corridor.

Tumbling through the door, Nashira fell to her hands and knees, closed her stinging eyes, and gasped in the warm air, coughing as it hit her throat. "Nashira?" someone asked. She opened her eyes and looked up.

Above her loomed a massive creature that appeared part-tyrannosaur, part-tarantula, part-rhinoceros, part-Sarlacc pit. Multiple tentacle-like tongues shot out from a gaping, cutlery-laden maw to sniff at her, while two of several pairs of muscular limbs reached toward her, spreading fearsome claws the size of her forearms.

Nashira sighed in relief at the familiar sight as those claws grasped her arms gently and helped her to her feet. "Thanks, Millie," she said. "Sorry, had a bit of a room mix-up."

"Oh, I understand, dear," Opmlqh said in soothing tones. "We're all used to it by now."

"Just be careful before you go into your room," Nashira told the Qhpong. "You don't want to get hit by the cold that got me."

"Why, whatever do you mean, Nashira? We're already in my room!"

Startled, the Hub scout looked around. Rather than the corridor, she stood in a room virtually identical to the one she'd just left, but furnished to accommodate Opmlqh's long-term tenancy, with a wide, padded sleeping bowl in the floor and an elaborate mini-abattoir for her live prey, one that still hadn't been fully cleaned from her latest repast. Nashira was distracted from that disturbing sight by her confusion. Could she have stumbled out into the corridor, tried again, and fallen into Room 5 without remembering it? "I didn't think I was *that* much out of it."

"What was that, sweetie?"

Nashira waved it off. "Nothing. Look, do you know if David's in his room?"

Opmlqh brightened. "Oh, yes, dear. He and his scrumptious boyfriend came home over an hour ago. They connected to my room too at first. They wouldn't stay, though."

That meant he and Julio would want to be alone. Still, warning David about the spy's imminent report was too important to put off. Nashira turned to leave.

Then she hesitated and turned back to the Qhpong. "Millie, tell me something."

"Anything, dear."

"How long have you been living here? It's at least five months, isn't it?"

"Just about," Opmlqh said. "I moved in a couple of weeks after David did, as I recall."

That was mildly suspicious right there. "It's odd for a species like yours to be living in a Hubstation meant for bipeds of roughly my size and biochemistry." Nashira gestured at the room around them. "These quarters must seem very cramped to you. I could understand if you were just passing through, but six months?"

It vaguely struck Nashira that it might be a bad idea to confront the massive, toothy predator if she actually were the Dosperhag's spy. But she was too pissed off by life in general right now to care much for such niceties.

Still, Opmlqh took the question in good spirits. "Why, that's simple, sweetie! Qhpong love cramped spaces. That's how our ancestors hunted—we'd dig out little caves and lie in wait for our prey. It helped protect us from the *big* carnivores." Nashira mentally added the Qhpong homeworld to her list of places to never, ever visit. "And I chose this Hubstation because its patrons' physiotype reminds me of my favorite prey, and your biochemical profile is just so exotic and savory. Most Qhpong don't appreciate the flavor, but I just can't get enough. Oh, I could just eat those long, meaty legs of yours right up if you'd let me, you scrumptious biped!" She tittered. "I'm sorry, that makes me sound like such a glutton."

"No, it's, ah, kind of flattering." Regardless of which way this conversation was heading, Nashira was eager to cut it short. "Look, I really have to be going."

"I understand, dear. But it was lovely getting to talk to you about something other than a male for a change!"

This time, Nashira kept her eyes wide open as she stepped out the door, through the subliminally brief, blurry limbo of the tesseract interface, then out the other side. This time, there was no ambiguity: rather than exiting into the corridor, she had stepped directly into another hotel room. "What?" This one was empty, its bedsheets not yet changed, but mercifully not freezing. Nashira turned back to the door, but the panel had already slid shut. She quickly slid it back open and stepped through. Once more, she emerged in a different room. "What the fuck is going on?"

Two faces, which had been huddled together in intimate conversation, looked up at her. One was that of a large-eyed amphibian biped with gold-green skin and a resplendent, backswept head crest in diaphanous red. The other was—

"Rynyan!" Nashira strode forward angrily. "What in hell are you doing here?"

"Oh, Nashira! What a lovely surprise. Have you met Yldai? She's a freelance sex worker from Druagomta. Isn't that lovely? I was surprised to find a member of such a noble profession working out of an... inexpensive hotel like this, but apparently she hasn't yet signed on with a proper franchise. I was just offering her my services as a reference—following an audition, of course. They know me quite well at all the best houses in the Hubcomplex."

Nashira dragged him away from the scantily clad amphibian. "Don't lie to me, Rynyan. I know why you're here. She's the Dospers' spy! You're here to get her report on David and pass it along to Morjepas like a good little quisling!"

Yldai puffed out her throat pouch in shock, causing its tattoos to expand into rather ribald forms. "Spy?! What are you talking about? Rynyan, who is this creature?"

"Just a simple misunderstanding, my lady," Rynyan said with a courtly bow. He pulled Nashira further into the entry alcove and whispered, "You wound me, Nashira, really. Yes, Morjepas did instruct me to receive the report. I suppose you overheard me—I thought I caught your enticing scent in my office before I left." He knew her by scent? She shuddered. "But I had no intention of following through. I came here to *warn*

David, just as you undoubtedly did. But then I ran into this charming young lady in the hallway, and we got to talking, and she invited me in, and, well..."

"And you forgot all about warning your friend because you couldn't resist a pretty... pouch?"

Rynyan gave her a wry look. "Is that really so unlike me, Nashira?"

He had a point. Still, Nashira stepped over to Yldai. "So how long have you been working out of this room?"

The Druagom gave an insouciant ripple of her flexible limbs. "A few weeks. Enough to get tired of the décor."

"So why are you still freelance? Lots of proper sex houses you could sign with."

"Criminal record," Yldai replied easily. "Juvenile stuff. Public molting, home-brew party religions, song transposing, the usual. But it makes it hard to break in at the legit places without a reputation."

Rynyan laughed. "Nashira, if you're insinuating that she's the spy, I think I would've known by now. After all, I did come here to meet the spy. Wouldn't she have told me?"

"Maybe she was biding her time to protect her cover. Maybe she really wants a reference from you." She shook her head. "All I know is, something weird's going on with the suite. We *both* need to get out of here and find David."

The bathroom door slid open as she spoke, and a Jiodeyn staggered out, dragging four heavy suitcases behind him. "Something is very wrong with this suite," he panted.

Rynyan stared. "Oh! You didn't tell me this was a threesome."

"It wasn't!" Yldai appeared quite shocked by the Jiodeyn's appearance. "Mr. Chojieg? How long have you been in my bathroom?"

"That's just it. I haven't! I've been trying to check out for some time now. But every time I go out the front door, I come back in to another room! I've been through every room in the suite by this point, some more than once. Last time I was back in my own room, I called the front desk to tell them. They're sending a maintenance crew." Chojieg looked around. "But this is the first time I've come through the *bathroom* door. Whatever the problem is, it's getting worse."

"Ridiculous," Rynyan said. "One of the first things I did when I took over was to order the suite interfaces repaired. We'll just see about this." He stepped past Chojieg and Yldai toward the bathroom door.

"Rynyan, wait!" Nashira ran after him. But he had already slid the door open and stepped through before she reached it. She caught it before it shut, seeing only a bewildering blur of overlapping, distorted images—which was odd, since she should be able to see clearly through the interface zone. Never mind that there was no dimensional interface on the *bathroom* door.

A moment later, Rynyan burst out of the jumble of images and into her arms, shivering mightily. "Wh-h-hooa-ah, it's cold in there!" His arms went around her.

"Rynyan!"

"Strictly for warmth, I promise."

"Get your bloody warmth somewhere else!" She shoved him away.

"I would, but Yldai's an ectotherm." He withered under her glare. "Anyway. Yes, something is anomalous here. No matter; I'll simply use my administrative code to reset the system." Moving to the front door, he popped open the access panel and entered the code. "There. That should do it!" He opened the door and strode confidently through the blur field.

"Oh, not again!" Nashira jumped through after him.

She emerged into a sea of noise and lights—one that seemed very much like a party. "I had no idea this suite was so lively!" Rynyan cried.

Nashira turned back, but the door had already slid shut. This time, it was the closet door. Hesitantly, she opened it again and leaned through the haze. Chojieg's empty room was on the other side.

"Oh, look, party crashers!" someone called.

Nashira turned, realizing that they were in the suite's double room. Since the cubic facet that served as the tesseract suite's entry interface was directly adjacent to only six of the other cubes, the eighth, opposing cube could only be reached by passing through one of the others. So the suite was divided into five single rooms and one double. Which made this room large enough to hold over a dozen people, mostly humans and mostly females. And mostly wasted, judging from the slurred voices and the bleary-eyed way they pawed at Rynyan, who was gladly letting himself be drawn into their spastic dancing.

The bronze-skinned, pink-haired woman who'd spoken took Nashira by the shoulders and went on in a slurred Brazilian accent. "I have no idea who you are, but you brought a Sosyryn! That's amazing! A Sosyryn slumming with humans!"

"Oh, you have no idea."

"I'm Mayte, what's your name?"

"Um... Nashira. Nashira Wing."

Mayte gasped. "That's so beautiful! With a name like that, you should be a space pilot!"

"Well... Hub scout."

"Oh, that's so glamorous! We're just flight crew from back home. Mostly the Earth-Hubpoint run, some tourist stuff, you know. We're here for the convention."

"And what is a convention without a room party?" asked another woman, a tall, elegant blonde with a heavy Russian accent. "Hello, *dahh*ling! I'm Anya, and I'm the host."

Nashira narrowed her eyes. For a human, it would be silly to suspect someone of being a spy just because she looked and sounded like she'd stepped out of a Bond movie. But the spy she sought had been hired by the Dosperhag, and aliens sometimes took human fictional tropes literally. Rynyan had once been convinced that the key to getting her laid was to impersonate a pizza delivery man. She might even have considered it if the pizza had been good enough.

"So this is your room?" she asked Anya.

"Just for the con."

"How long have you been here?"

"Couple of days. We go back to the grind tomorrow, so this is our last chance to party down Hub-style!"

"Why choose this room?"

"It was the right size, and it was affordable." Anya gasped. "Oh, no, don't you like it? I want all my guests to be happy!"

The door signal sounded, and Anya brightened. "Oh! There are more now! Be right back."

"What? Wait! The door!"

Nashira took a step, but Mayte blocked her path, smiling seductively. "Hub scouting sounds so adventurous! You have to tell me all about it."

"Later, okay?" She shoved past. Another pair of humans was coming through the door—and Nashira had never been so overjoyed to see the ugly decorative pattern of the corridor wallpaper. "Coming through!" she cried, trying to push past the newcomers before the door closed, ignoring their complaints.

But the door was already sliding shut. She shot a hand out to wedge into the crack, but only got a chipped fingernail for her trouble. She immediately hit the opening control and ducked through—but a blast of devastating cold struck her in the face and she fell back.

Anya and her guests had already moved deeper into the room, forgetting her. She looked for Rynyan and found him making out with Mayte, who appeared even more aggressive about it than he was. Nashira pulled him away with some difficulty, then described what had just occurred. "So people can come into the suite, but they can't get out."

"Oh. That could become an issue."

"How could this be happening? Not just getting trapped here, but even the bathroom and closet doors connecting? There's no way the interface *could* connect to an inside door, is there? I mean, if it could, there'd be no need for a double room."

"Well, yes and no. In the simplest, four-dimensional sense, no, such connections don't exist. But the tesseract is being projected down into three-dimensional space. If you rotate that projection, the different facets do appear to pass through one another. In theory, I suppose you could exploit that overlap to join any two points within the tesseract, although the interface needs a solid framework like a doorway to latch onto. But it would require a more elaborate dimensional manifold than the rooms are equipped with."

"Could the spy be doing this?"

"Why would they? They were supposed to come to me to

report. Now they're trapped in here with the rest of us."

Nashira frowned. "And we're trapped in here with them. And there's no telling which of the guests it is."

"Surely not Millie!"

"She's been here the longest—moved in just after David. She has an excuse—they all do—but any one of them could be lying."

"But Mr. Chojieg, Anya—They're just here for a few days."

"That could be a cover too. Change up the agents, avoid suspicion." She peered up at him. "Assuming you don't already know who it is. For someone who says he came here to warn David, you don't seem very keen on finding him."

"But there are just so many lovely diversions. I'm only Sosyryn. Besides, you're here! You always save David. So my involvement at this point is somewhat redundant, don't you think?"

Admittedly, if he were sincerely going behind the Dosperhag's backs, he would need plausible deniability. And if he were lying...

"You're right—you'd better stay here, out of the way. Where it's safe." *For me and David, at least.*

"Of course." Rynyan beamed as the female partygoers pulled him back toward the dance floor. "I understand perfectly. If you need me, you know where I'll be!"

"Right," Nashira muttered. "But getting back here could be a problem."

Well, there was nothing for it but to try. At this point, she'd been in every room *except* David's, so the odds were in her favor. With that in mind, she took a deep breath, opened the front door, and stepped through the blur field, keeping one hand on the door frame to hold it open just in case.

The distortion cleared, and she saw a room from the perspective of the bathroom door. There, at last, right in front of her, was David.

And Julio.

In bed.

Naked.

And...

...

Her brain didn't start working again until she heard Mayte's voice alongside her. "Wow, Anya, you didn't tell us it would be *this* kind of party!"

9

David and Julio both looked up in shock as more female partygoers filed through the door Nashira had held open, gasping and squealing in approval at the sight. David leapt out of bed with a girlish yelp—incongruously so, Nashira thought as she sized him up—and looked around for something to cover himself with. He grabbed a large, oddly shaped silver box on the bedside table and held it over his nether regions. "Oh, don't stop on our account!" Anya cried.

Julio had also climbed out of bed, but by contrast, he was standing calmly and confidently naked while the admiring partygoers looked on. "Ladies! Your attention flatters me, but you should know I'm strictly into my fellow man."

Mayte grinned. "That's just what we're here to see!"

Julio's gaze was colder as it turned to Nashira. "Is that what you're here for too? Hiding in our bathroom to spy on us?"

"No, I—it's—you don't seem to mind!"

"Where my body's concerned, I've got no cause for shame. But what David and I share is not for your amusement. You had your chance with him, and you didn't take it. Don't imagine that you're entitled to him now."

"That's not what—I wasn't—Look, you need to listen, there's a lot going on and—" She broke off, for the still-embarrassed David had inched his way over to the closet door and was now ducking inside to hide. "No, David, don't let the door close!"

Nashira pushed past Julio as the engineer turned and cried, "The closet, David? That's so old-fashioned!" Ignoring him, Nashira reached the closet door just in time to see David's adorable bare bum diffusing into the blur field. She squeezed through the door just before it slid shut behind her...

...and collided full-on with David from behind, for he had pulled up short at the sight of Chojieg's vacant room. Startled, David stumbled forward and spun, struggling to keep the rhombus-faced box strategically positioned in front of him.

"Nashira!"

She choked down a giggle. "Sorry."

"Are you really? How long were you watching us?"

"I didn't mean to! I just... I came out and there you both were and I just... lost track."

"How long?"

"Well... long enough to see you do that thing with... and then you both... Bloody hell, David, I had no idea you were that limber."

"Nashira!"

"It's a compliment! You should be flattered."

He blushed. "It's not about me, Nashira. I don't... I don't mind you seeing me naked," he said, though his taut grip on the box belied his words. "It's... well, it's only fair. You should know... there was this time, back on Renziov when your towel slipped and..."

She laughed. "I know, silly. I was seeing if I could get a rise out of you. But you didn't have enough of a clue to notice you were being flirted with, so you missed your chance."

"Oh. Um..." He shook it off. "Like I was saying, it's not about me. You embarrassed Julio. Intruded on something private." Nashira couldn't argue, recalling Julio's very similar words. "I knew he was insecure about you and me," David continued, "but I didn't know why until now. I thought we were just good friends."

She stepped closer. "And now that you know better?"

"It doesn't change anything. You—you should've said something before. I would've... I would've been honored to be with a woman as smart and brave and beautiful as you. But Julio's just as beautiful, and maybe even smarter, and he actually laughs at my jokes. I love him. I love you too, as a friend, but he's the person I'm with."

Hearing him say those three words to her, even with the

equivocation, burned like the air in the frozen room. No one had ever said that to her and meant it like David had, even platonically. It drove her onward. "He's the *man* you're with," she said. "I'm a woman." She pulled off her tank top to illustrate that. "So... would it even count as cheating?"

"It doesn't work that way," he said with gentle apology. "Not for me."

"How do you know until you try?" Her trousers hit the floor.

David pulled back a few steps. "Nashira, please. This isn't like you."

"No, it isn't. But you know what? I'm fucking sick of being me." She went to work on her bra clasp. "I never liked being me. Until you came along. And you liked me. You were nice to me!" She tossed her bra aside fiercely. "I couldn't make sense of that at first, so I pushed you away. I didn't deserve someone to be that kind to me. But you kept being kind. You believed in me. You gave me hope. And I liked it. Got used to having it around." Wrapping her arms around his neck, she finished, "And you know what? I just decided I'm not about to let it get away."

She pulled his head down and kissed him fiercely, deeply. After a moment, his hands tentatively moved around her back; the box remained sandwiched between them. Nashira reached down to pull it away.

David caught himself and broke free. "No! I'm sorry, Nashira, but this is wrong. Whatever we could've had... it's too late now."

His words hit her like a slap. Realizing what she was doing, she sank down to sit on the side of the bed and hugged her knees in front of her. She felt tears stinging her eyes. "I'm sorry."

David sat by her at a platonic distance, held the box in his lap, and laid a hand on her shoulder. "You can tell me what's going on."

She struggled to organize the litany of her anxieties. The frustrations the vector list had brought in place of the triumph she'd longed for; the loneliness of diving without David by her side; the fear of losing her one true friend to Julio and Tsshar; and now the threat that the Dosperhag might make another attempt on David's life without Nashira there to protect him. It had all piled up on her at once and driven her to this moment of desperation. It humiliated her that she'd let her feelings for David make her lose control. But at the same time, she knew that if she explained all this, he would understand and forgive her. And maybe that, not sex, was what she really needed from him right now.

Nashira leaned against him and lowered her head onto his shoulder. He tensed for a moment, then relaxed into it and stretched his arm comfortingly across her back. "Thank you," she breathed, eyes moistening. "I needed this. I've just been so—"

"David! What the hell?"

David and Nashira both jumped up and spun to see a wide-eyed Julio staring at them—mercifully wearing pants this time. David fumbled the box and let it fall. "This isn't what it looks like!" he cried.

"Oh, it had better not be!"

Nashira reflexively grabbed the box off the floor and held it in front of her own crotch. A moment later, realizing how ridiculous she was being, she handed the box back to David. "We were just talking, I promise. I got a little carried away, okay, but it's fine now." Straightening her knickers, she looked around for the rest of her clothes, but she'd tossed them all over the far half of the room, behind Julio.

"I don't think it's for you to decide whether it's fine," Julio told her.

"I just meant—"

The front door slid open and the cleaning robot emerged, frost forming on its frigid surface as it hit the warm, moist air of Chojieg's room. It paused for a moment, disoriented, then clicked back into its program. "Excuse me. This room is about to be cleaned and reconfigured for new tenancy. Environmental conditions will be in flux. Please depart for your comfort and safety."

Even as it continued its precautionary spiel, the robot rolled forward, deploying its cleaning arms menacingly. Julio retreated to the back of the room alongside the others. "No, stop!" Nashira cried as the robot picked up her clothes and dropped them in its trash receptacle.

But the robot didn't stop. Either it was deranged by the room anomaly, or it was as badly maintained as everything else in this fleatrap. It began to deploy caustic cleaning sprays, forcing the three humans with one pair of trousers among them to retreat into the bathroom.

They emerged from a closet and found their way blocked by the spiny back of a Baiukua, dozens of ultra-sharp pinpoints just millimeters from Nashira's bare chest. She'd never been so grateful for her slender figure. She and David hastened to back away into the room, only to find themselves met with Opmlqh's equally sharp claws and fangs.

"Oh, hello, you three! My, you look like you've been having fun!"

David gasped. "Will someone tell me what's going on?"

"Just a little malfunction with the dimensional interface," the Qhpong assured him. "Mr. Hevhuo here has been working on it, and I'm sure he'll have everything repaired in no time."

"That's how I ended up in your bathroom door," Nashira explained to the men. "I was coming to warn you, there's—" She broke off, still unsure about Opmlqh's bona fides.

Julio looked intrigued. "You mean the manifold has become randomized? Nexus surfaces are forming between any two doors?"

"If that means people can get in but not out, then, yeah."

The dreadlocked engineer stared at David. "The safe! David, that's how *it* works! Without the proper combination, nothing placed inside it can be retrieved. Somehow, the room interface is mimicking the safe's interface."

Nashira didn't know what safe he was referring to, but the spiny maintenance worker moved in to examine the box in David's hands. "Octacube safe, eh? Those are rare. First one I've seen."

"So you don't know how to fix it?" David asked.

"Only the obvious. If it's the problem, then it's gotta go." He yanked it out of David's grip, opened the front door, and rolled it out.

"No! Artie's in there!" The naked young man lunged out after it. Nashira followed, vainly hoping that the safe's removal would somehow fix everything and she'd end up in the corridor. At this point, she'd gladly parade through the entire Hubstation in her knickers if it meant she could put this awful day behind her.

No such luck. They emerged back in Yldai's room. Chojieg was drowsing on the couch, wearing only a bathrobe and looking far more relaxed than when Nashira had last seen him. The amphibian sex worker herself, no doubt the author of Chojieg's contentment, was not in evidence. "She's in the bathroom," Chojieg murmured. "Or... somewhere. Could be anywhere by now. One of these doors must lead *into* a bathroom..."

Julio slipped through the front door before it shut. He knelt to study the safe that David had once again positioned for modesty. "This doesn't make sense. I... retrieved the safe from Tsshar's cargo module, which is also a tesseract. So just having this in here shouldn't be causing this. There must be something linking them somehow. Some kind of transdimensional field."

"What could cause that?" David asked.

Nashira checked the closet to see if there was another bathrobe, but she found only the interface haze. "Shit."

"Hard to say without more information," Julio replied. "Must be some apparatus that someone in here is operating. We'd have to go through the rooms, ask everyone what they have."

"All my stuff's in my suitcases," Chojieg muttered, pointing to the pile of luggage that took up most of one corner of the room. "Nothing's powered up. And I don't have any trans-whatevers."

"All right," Julio said. "I'll circulate around the suite and talk to the tenants." He hesitated, eyes moving between David and Nashira. Reluctantly, he said, "You two stay here. We don't want you hitting the cold room. I'll try to bring you some clothes in a bit."

Nashira met his eyes. "Good luck."

Julio nodded. Taking a deep breath, he triggered the front door and stepped into the haze.

A second later, the closet door slid open and Julio emerged into the very entry hall he'd just vacated. "Huh. Well, luck of the draw." Chuckling, he reopened the closet door and stepped through it.

A second later, the bathroom door slid open, and Nashira spun to see Julio emerging. "It seems we have a new problem," the engineer said.

"Great," Nashira groaned. "So we're trapped in this room now?"

"Do you think everyone's trapped in their rooms?" David wondered.

The closet door slid open, disgorging Yldai. "Oh, no, not you again," she said, retreating back into the closet before the door shut. A few moments later, she emerged from the bathroom door behind Julio. "What? I tried a different door!"

At that moment, Mayte and another woman and man from the party came in through the front door. The pink-haired Brazilian took in the room's occupants in their various states of undress and beamed. "Now this is a real party! Everybody get naked!" She whipped off her loose blouse.

"The effect is converging on this room now," Julio said. "It started when we brought the octacube in. So the source of the transdimensional field must be here too."

Nashira stared at Yldai. "So you *must* be the spy!"

"What spy?" David asked.

"Why do you keep saying that?!" the Druagom cried. "Maybe you're the spies—carrying around a high-security safe like that!"

"Oh, we're playing spies now?" slurred Mayte, now fully nude. "Shoulda told me before I blew my cover!" Nashira ducked around her and snagged her discarded blouse from the floor. It was trashy, but it was coverage.

Rynyan, escorting Anya and another human woman, emerged from the bathroom door just as Nashira pulled on the blouse. "Oh-h, what did I just miss?" he moaned.

Nashira confronted him. "Yldai *is* the spy. And you came to meet her!"

"What spy?" David asked.

The Baiukua maintenance man, Hevhuo, emerged through the front door. The eleven other occupants crowded back to avoid his spines, but there wasn't room to move very far. "Don't worry, folks, my instruments have localized the problem to this room. I've called for my assistant, and we should be resolving this shortly."

"No, not more people!" Nashira cried—just as three more partygoers popped in through two doors.

Julio pushed through the growing crowd to speak to Hevhuo. "We're looking for a transdimensional field generator of some kind."

"Oh, I have just the thing!" Hevhuo rummaged through his toolbelt and retrieved a probe. The crowd did what little it could to part around him as he scanned the room. Nashira pressed herself against several partygoers to evade his spines, not trusting in Mayte's flimsy blouse to protect her.

"This is ridiculous," Yldai insisted. "I'm no spy, I keep telling you!"

"What spy?!" David demanded.

"Ah, I've got something!" Hevhuo's tracker had led him to Chojieg's piled luggage. He withdrew a thick, rectangular crystal slab from the side pouch of the largest bag. "Let's just see what this does..."

No change was immediately evident when he activated it, but then Mayte gasped in awe. "Oh-h, the walls are changing!"

It wasn't a hallucination kicking in, since Nashira could see it too. Superimposed on the wall décor of Yldai's room was a different set of wall decorations that the Hub scout recognized. "How did we get back in my room?" David wondered.

"We didn't," Julio said, taking the device from Hevhuo. He worked its controls for a moment, and suddenly another David came in through the door, walked clear through several of the room's occupants including the first David, and sat down on the bed to talk to his computer fish, whose tank had appeared on Yldai's bedside table overlapping personal effects whose nature Nashira did not want to know. With the touch of another control, Julio changed the image to one of David and Nashira arguing—or rather, Nashira arguing and David replying with patient good humor.

"It's taking advantage of the tesseract geometry," Julio said. "All the rooms are projected within a single 3-D volume. Effectively they occupy the same space at once. This device makes the dimensional boundary transparent. And it's been recording events in David's room for months."

"And it was in your luggage!" Yldai cried, pointing at Chojieg.

"That's absurd," the Jiodeyn replied. "I haven't been here for months."

"They could've swapped out agents to keep their cover," Nashira countered.

"I've been through every room in this suite. Anyone could've planted it in my bag when I was distracted. That Qhpong insisted on preparing me a snack—or *as* a snack, I wasn't sure—and the partygoers tried to make me dance with them. Come to think of it, that Anya woman tried to take my luggage."

"It was crowding my guests!" the Russian hostess protested.

"Did someone mention me?" Opmlqh pushed her way in through the front door, forcing everyone back into Hevhuo's spines, which in turn forced them the other way.

"You see what I mean?" Anya gasped as she was squished in the middle.

"Sorry to barge in," said the Qhpong, "but I thought that if we're stuck in here for a while, I should make snacks."

"No need, Millie," Rynyan called over the heads of the crowd. "I ordered room service for the party. It should be here any—oh, dear."

"We have to get the hell out of here!" Nashira cried.

"We have all the pieces now," Julio said. "We just need to break the safe combination and—"

"Is Hevhuo in here?" Another set of hedgehog spines pushed in through the front door. "I'm his assistant."

Rynyan chuckled. "Oh, why not? Come on in! The more, the merrier!"

"Hurry!" Nashira cried.

"Who breaks my safe?" Tsshar scurried through the legs of the room's occupants, knocking Nashira into Mayte's lap as the naked partygoer tried to make out with Chojieg on the loveseat. "I track my safe here, and I find all you people. Who takes it from me?"

Julio and David pointed at each other. "He did it," they both said. Tsshar snatched her safe away from David, leaving him fully exposed. Several girls from the party shrieked in approval, and David retreated behind Julio for cover.

"Doesn't matter," Nashira cried, pulling away from Mayte's attempts to make out with her. "Tsshar, that safe has trapped us all in this suite. You have to shut it down."

"Not yet!" Julio said. "We need to match the spy field device to its exact dimensional calibration at the moment David and I triggered the safe's randomization. We have to find the right moment in its replay. Tsshar, you have to enter the safe combination exactly then."

"With all these watchers? Never!"

"Wait," Nashira said. "If we let everyone out, then the spy will get away."

"Will someone explain to me about the spy?" David moaned.

"Oh, it's quite simple," Rynyan said.

Something pushed the crowd closer together; Nashira couldn't even see who it was now. "Excuse me, I'm Yolien, the assistant manager. Are my maintenance people in here?"

"Who *isn't* in here?" Chojieg complained.

Julio knelt by Tsshar. "Look, Captain, there's no choice. This is our only way out. I'll cue up the spy device, you open the safe, okay?"

"No! *My* safe! Private! No one sees the combination!"

The sound of the door opening filled Nashira with dread. "Room service! Did you order the eight jumbo party platters?"

"Oh, that's me!" Rynyan called. "Bring them right on in!"

"Rynyan!" several people cried at once.

"Well, I'm not going to send all these bellhops away without tipping them!"

It was getting hard to breathe now. David yelped as his bum had a close encounter with several of Hevhuo's spines. "Come on, Tsshar!" Nashira gasped. "Nobody can see your fucking combination anyway!"

"No!" Tsshar had clambered up onto the trays the bellhops carried over their heads. "No Mrwadj gives away a secret to so many! Never!"

The bathroom door opened once more. Nashira's heart

raced at the whir of the cleaning robot's motors. "Excuse me. This room is about to be cleaned and reconfigured for new tenancy..."

Julio tried to force the robot back through the door, and soon David and Hevhuo joined him. But it was a losing battle. "Come on, Tsshar!" Julio cried as the robot forced its way farther inside, beginning to deploy its spray nozzles. The chain reaction through the crowd forced Opmlqh to rear up on her hind limbs, crowding the ceiling and leaving little room even for Tsshar.

"Oh, all right!" the Mrwadj cried. "Set the device!"

"Everyone, try to clear a space by the bed," Julio said, letting Hevhuo's assistant take over against the cleaning robot.

"Right," Rynyan quipped. "I'll just call the desk and have them send up a fifth dimension."

It was easier said than done, but enough people were able to squeeze close and climb on top of each other (a process Mayte audibly enjoyed) to open a space for Julio to play back the scene of himself and David working on the safe. "You put your fish in to crack it from inside?" Tsshar asked when the playback reached that point. "Clever."

David barely had room to shrug. "Until it closed and we lost him."

"Bad execution. Good idea."

"Start entering the combination now, Tsshar!" Julio cried. "Trigger in five, four, three, two, one... *now!*"

The cleaning robot squealed. Its cleanly severed front half fell back into the bathroom, which was finally visible through the door. Whoever was standing by the front entrance hit the panel and cried in triumph. The room's twenty-plus occupants cheered as the crowding began to diminish.

Then Nashira remembered herself. "David, the spy! We can't let the tenants leave!"

"Oh, of course we can," Rynyan said as the hotel staffers began organizing an orderly evacuation. "As I was trying to tell you, Nashira, you were right the first time. Yldai is the spy."

Nashira stared. "You knew?"

"Of course!" Julio said. "Why didn't I see it? She knew the

octacube was a safe. How could a low-level sex worker recognize such a rare, high-grade security device?"

"But we talked about it in her room," David said.

"Before she got back," Julio replied. Nashira realized he was right.

Rynyan preened his feathers. "Well, sure, if you wanted to figure it out the hard way."

Julio stared. "What tipped *you* off?"

"Quite simple, my good man. Her tattoos mark her as a member of the 893rd Spawning. The Druagom's last law against public molting was repealed by the 889th Spawning, before she was even born!"

Chojieg laughed in relief. "Of course! It was so obvious."

"All right!" Yldai cried. "You found me out. But you won't stop me!" She produced a weapon from somewhere on her scantily clad form and waved it menacingly at the thinning crowd. She couldn't reach the spy device, but she moved for the door anyway, pushing past the remaining occupants. "Keep it. I have a copy right here. The Dosperhag will be intrigued to learn about you humans and your secret undertaki—*hukk!*"

Yldai convulsed and collapsed, and Opmlqh withdrew a lengthy, dripping tongue back into her mouth. "Don't worry, dears, she's just anaesthetized. Oh, and the venom from that particular tongue causes short-term memory loss. I gave her enough that she should forget being found out. Is that okay?"

Nashira sighed. "Yeah, Millie. That's very okay. Hell, feel free to bite off her arm or leg if you feel like it."

Opmlqh drew back, scandalized. "Without consent? I could never!"

While the confused assistant manager instructed a departing bellhop to summon a stretcher for Yldai, David remembered his nudity and ducked behind Chojieg's piled luggage for concealment. But then he caught the Sosyryn's eye. "Rynyan. I'm not sure what just happened here, but... did you save me from something?"

Rynyan smiled at him with warmth and relief. "Of course, my friend. I won't let you down ever again."

"Well... we'll have to wait and see. It can be hard to know

who I can rely on," he finished with a glance toward Nashira.

The Hub scout wanted to apologize for her seduction attempt and explain what had motivated it. But there were still too many people around.

"Here," Tsshar said, coming up to David and handing him Art's tank, which she'd retrieved from her safe. "I normally don't give things, but… I don't earn this today. You do. Going for my most private safe—brazen. I like."

"Tsshar, I can't…" Julio glared at him, but David went on. "I can't take credit."

"For taking the safe? Of course not. Julio takes it. He's the last person I let in—you think I'm stupid?" The engineer looked sheepish. "But I watch the playback. Your idea to use the fish. Your idea to buy the fish. Starting to think, use resources. We make a thief of you yet!" She looked him over. "Also, being naked confounds pickpockets. A clever play."

Tsshar bounded from the room with her safe, leaving David with Art's tank, which he used to cover himself anew. "Man," David said. "This has been the most embarrassing night of my life. What a relief it's nearly over." Nashira didn't have the heart to point out that a clear tank of nutrient fluid and bioengineered piscid did more to magnify than conceal.

She was distracted by laughter and joyous whooping from Mayte, Anya, and the remaining party guests, who had gathered around the bed. "Oh, no," Julio moaned as the women grew more raucous. "I left the playback on."

He and David circled to get a better look, and Nashira followed. Indeed, the playback of recent events in David's room—and on David's bed—had caught up to the early stages of the activity that Nashira had interrupted. Rendered in perfect dimensional fidelity, as if it were happening live in front of them—which, in a larger spatiotemporal sense, it was.

"Man," David said after a few dumbstruck moments. "I *am* limber."

10

The throbbing of Nashira's head woke her up. She had a killer hangover, and she was naked in an unfamiliar bed. None of that surprised her, after the wreck the previous day had been.

Climbing out of bed, she blinked in the bright light coming through the windows and wondered how she'd ended up in such a swanky place. The room was incredibly large and ornate, and rather than being a tesseract suite (thank Heaven), it looked like a residence in one of the high-class, terraformed habitat rings. *Who did I go to bed with last night?*

She struggled to recall. After the mess with the hotel suite, once she'd assessed the damage she'd done to her friendship with David and the total lack of other real friends in her life, she'd wanted only to torture herself. She didn't deserve a lover as kind and generous as David and Julio had been to each other. So she'd sought out the most depraved, humiliating sexual experience she could find, one so odious that it might cover up the disgust she felt toward her other recent actions. It could only have been...

"Ohh, fuck, no."

"Good morning!" Rynyan crowed, looking refreshed and chipper as he strode into the room wearing a dressing gown that cost more than Nashira earned in a year. "Or good afternoon, actually. You really earned a good morning's sleep last night, I must say."

She had slept with Rynyan.

It was the one thing she had sworn up and down that she would never do. The one thing she'd wanted less than to spend the rest of her life as a Hub scout. It had been barely a month since she'd finally convinced him it would never happen. Yet at her lowest ebb, she had done it anyway...

And...

It had been the most amazing night of her life.

She remembered now. Despite Rynyan's arrogance and self-absorption, he had been an astonishingly kind and generous lover. He had devoted himself diligently and passionately to her pleasure, placing it above his own at every turn. He had listened to her more attentively, responded to her needs more considerately, understood her body more expertly, and read her responses more sensitively than anyone she'd ever slept with. He had kept her in nearly constant ecstasy for hours, then done it again after an hour of comforting her gently while she sobbed out years' worth of pent-up loneliness and pain into his soft-feathered mane. And his body was... she had no words. All those boasts over the years about his sexual prowess, his anatomy, his ability to satisfy any female's greatest desires—every last word had been true. If anything, he'd been modest.

I should've realized, she thought. Sosyryn prided themselves on their generosity, defined their wealth by how much they gave. Even if Rynyan's performance had been motivated by his egotistical need to be the most generous lover in the galaxy, he was still... just about the most generous lover in the galaxy. No one had ever made Nashira feel so valued, so special, so important. It had been exactly what she'd needed in her darkest hour.

And she wanted more.

Grinning, forgetting her hangover, Nashira slinked toward the beautiful Sosyryn and put her arms around his neck, enjoying how his mane feathers tickled her forearms. "I'm glad you liked it, Ryns. I have to say... if I'd known it would be like that, I never would've turned you down." She kissed him, enjoying the fine furriness of his muzzle. "And I'm gonna say 'yes' a hell of a lot more from now on."

After another kiss, Rynyan gingerly pushed her away. "Ah. Yes. About that, Nashira... I'm very gratified that you found our evening so fulfilling, but I'm afraid it's best if we resume our usual, platonic relationship from now on."

Nashira gaped, stunned. "What?! You... This has been your bloody Holy Grail for years! Now just once and it's 'let's be friends?' Come on, you once said it'd be weeks at least before you got tired of me."

"Well, I *am* your supervisor, after all, so it's not really ethical, is it? I made an exception last night because you were so insistent, and, well, I was weak. But my newfound respect for you demands that I behave appropriately toward you from now on."

"Screw that! You never met a rule you couldn't bribe your way past! You're a Sosyryn! You can have anything you want! And now this is finally on the list!" she finished, gesturing toward her crotch.

Rynyan fidgeted, as though trying to break news gently. "That's just the thing, Nashira. You see... I've never had to delay gratification for anything as long as I have for sex with you. And the anticipation... Well, I imagined such wonders. So many incredible fantasies for so long. Oh, you were perfectly adequate, mind you. Excellent, in fact—allowing for your chemical impairment. But next to the extraordinary things I've imagined over the years... I'm afraid I was a bit underwhelmed by the reality. You understand, I'm sure."

Nashira sank onto the luxurious bed, barely noticing its softness. She didn't even know how to process being frustrated in such an intense desire she'd known so briefly. Finally, she laughed. Falling back onto the bed, she shook it with long, bitter paroxysms of hilarity at the sheer patheticness of Nashira Wing.

"Oh, I'm so pleased you're all right with it!" Rynyan said. "That should facilitate our working relationship going forward. And, um... I'm afraid I'm going to need the room."

She sat up on her elbows. "Come again?"

"As I said, you slept rather late. I have another rendezvous scheduled for—right now, actually. You might want to leave before she arrives."

Nashira sighed in resignation as she sat up. "Why? Jealous type?"

"No, but... you might find it a bit awkward if..."

"Hello, little human!" Tsshar bounded into the room and landed on Nashira's shoulders and chest, six sets of tiny, sharp claws poking into her bare skin. "I see you learn David's no-pocket trick. You win this round!"

COUNT THREE

HUBSTITUTE CREATURES

11

"I don't know what more I can tell you, Morjepas," Rynyan said to the quantelope in his office's communications shack. "As I explained last week, your spy delivered the report to me, then we had fairly brief but intense sex, during which she employed certain intoxicants in quantities that, in combination with my mind-altering lovemaking, caused a degree of memory loss. It was quite annoying to go to all that trouble for her and have her forget the whole thing. Fortunately, she allowed me to repeat my performance before taking her new job at Hyrynyz Pleasure City." At least the last sentence of that was true, aside from the "repeat" part. Rynyan had disliked telling Yldai that they'd made love when they actually hadn't yet; he had always prided himself on being scrupulously honest and forthright about his desires and intentions with all his potential and actual sexual partners. He took comfort in the knowledge that it was what *would* have happened, at Yldai's own invitation, if Nashira hadn't interrupted them in the Druagom's room.

"A job that you recommended her for," the quantelope replied in Morjepas's suspicious voice.

"Well, her audition was—they *both* were very memorable for me. And it was what she wanted most. I can't help it if she valued her career in the erotic arts more than her little side job for you. And I *did* send you the report, so my part in that sordid business was concluded." Admittedly, Yldai's subsequent performance hadn't been *quite* good enough to meet Hyrynyz's elevated standards, but the intensive training program there would surely compensate for that. And offering her a job at one of the Network's most esteemed pleasure cities had been an effective way to silence any lingering doubts or questions in Yldai's mind, and to prevent her from comparing notes with the Dosperhag about the contents of her report. Hyrynyz courtesans were in great demand, and the waiting list even to speak to them was booked up for years in advance.

"You sent a corrupted file with extensive irregularities and gaps in the data, revealing nothing of value."

"No doubt the result of the interference between her transdimensional sensor and the tesseract interface. It's not my problem if your people use flawed methods. Now, if you don't mind, I smell someone in my office. I really need to get back to work." He almost managed to get out the word "work" without audible disgust. His decision to stick with the manager job had proven detrimental to the recent rehabilitation of his image; many who would normally have come to him in search of charity were now becoming suspicious of why a Sosyryn needed to work for a living, and were starting to take their requests to his rivals instead. Penance, it turned out, could be quite inconvenient.

"Very well, Manager Zynara. But that work will be under increased scrutiny hereforth. If you fail us again, it will *become* your problem."

Morjepas signed off unhappily, though Rynyan was rather happier to recognize the human male scent wafting into the shack. Stepping out into the office, he spread his arms and cried, "David! How wonderful to see you again."

David nodded a bit uneasily. "Rynyan. I, uh, I overheard that. You really made sure Yldai was out of the picture?"

"Of course, David. And I edited her recordings to remove any incriminating details the Dosperhag could use against you or Nashira."

David blushed. "Did you edit out the sex parts?"

"Oh, I wouldn't have dared to tamper with such impressive performances! Rest assured that every second of your lovemaking with Julio will now be preserved in official Network records for the benefit of posterity. Not that the Dosperhag are likely to appreciate the show as much as Anya and her friends did."

The young human fidgeted and cleared his throat. It was endearing how shy he always was about accepting praise.

"Well... I am grateful that... that you looked out for me."

Rynyan spoke tentatively. "I know it doesn't make up for what I did before. But I am trying."

"I know you are."

"Then... are we friends again?"

David's response was slow. "I'm willing to give it a try."

"Wonderful!" Rynyan pulled him into a hug. David returned it only hesitantly, but even that was a relief. "Honestly, I could use a friend right now," Rynyan told him. "I'm afraid I've had a bit of a... well, a misunderstanding with Nashira."

David frowned. "What do you mean?"

Rynyan led him over to the couch, weighing his words. For once, he was reluctant to boast about a sexual encounter; in order to spare Nashira's feelings, he chose to keep quiet about her underwhelming lovemaking. He knew it wasn't quite fair to judge what had honestly been a more than adequate performance against his heightened expectations, but that was exactly why he didn't trust himself to sing her praises.

"Let's just say that I tried to do her a favor and somehow managed to hurt her feelings—not for the first time, I admit. Since then, she's thrown herself into pursuing that silly vector list to the exclusion of almost everything else. Well, I did persuade her to train the new scout I finally found to replace Mansura. He is a rather handsome human, and I hoped she'd take him to bed—a gift of sorts from me, to make amends for... well, what happened between us. But she's been all business about it. The list is the only thing she shows any passion for. And the longer she goes without it paying off, the more frustrated she gets. I'm worried about her, David. Maybe if you talked to her..."

David grew uneasy. "I'm the wrong person to ask, Rynyan. I've had a 'misunderstanding' with her too. And she was the one who hurt my feelings, and Julio's." He fidgeted. "To be honest, I think she feels bad about it. She's been avoiding me. But... well, I'm not sure I mind her avoiding me right now."

Rynyan smiled. It was endearing how little understanding humans had of their own emotions. David was trying to be angry and aloof, but it was obvious how much he missed Nashira.

"Oh, come now, David," Rynyan said gently. "You're... well,

you're you. If you could find it in your heart to forgive me for almost getting your planet attacked by an evil conspiracy, then surely you can forgive whatever Nashira's done."

The young human blinked. "Well, when you put it that way..." After a moment, he sighed. "I'll think about it, but it'll have to wait. *Miifu*'s heading out in a few hours. That's why I'm here, to update our flight clearance. We're taking out a passenger on this trip."

Rynyan's spirits sank. "So you didn't just come here to see me?"

David offered a small smile. "I didn't have to do it in person."

Reassured, Rynyan led him over to the desk and took care of the clearance update. "There you are. I hope you and Julio have a wonderful trip."

"Looks like Julio isn't coming this time," David said with a puzzled frown. "Tsshar won't tell me where he is, but she says he should be back in a few days."

"Oh, that's too bad."

"Well, I have other friends in the crew."

"But not lovers. That's why I never limit myself to fewer than three at a time." He grinned. "Often literally."

David halted by the door. "Oh, that reminds me. I wanted to ask you for some romantic advice. You know my crewmate Jojjimok?"

"The strapping young Hijjeg fellow?"

"That's him. Turns out he has a bit of a crush on Millie from my hotel suite. I've been trying to talk him into asking her out, but he's really shy. Maybe you could give me some pointers on building his confidence."

Rynyan's eyes widened. "A Hijjeg and a Qhpong? That's quite a lot of limbs." Even with all his experience with interspecies sex, he had trouble imagining the topology of that pairing—though it would be fun to try. "I can't blame the lad for being intimidated. But you just remind him what a sweetheart Millie is. I'm sure she'd be happy to give him a chance."

"Do you think Millie would mind that he's an herbivore?" David asked.

"Not at all! She finds herbivores delicious."

Vivek Dhawan pushed the Hubdiver's thruster controls to full power, aiming for the glimmer of laser light that emanated from the middle of nowhere—though it was about to be in the middle of something far more impassable. With every second, the smoldering orange clouds of the oncoming brown dwarf loomed closer in the display wall.

"Pull up," Nashira Wing advised. "You'll never make it in time."

"No!" the younger man insisted. "I won't be stranded here!"

But it was too late. The laser beacon that marked the Hubpoint vanished within the dense clouds before the *Starship Entropy* could reach it. Snarling in frustration, Vivek veered off and tried to pull out of his dive—but it was too late to prevent the scout ship from plunging into the dwarf's incandescent atmosphere at lethal speed.

Nashira smacked the back of Vivek's head. "Congratulations—we're not stranded," she said as the simulation ended and the Entropy's display wall returned to the normal view of its docking bay in Hubstation 3742. "We're just dead. For the fourteenth time."

"Well, what else could we do?" the trainee Hub scout asked, rubbing his head. "The Hubpoint is our only way back to civilization!"

"What, did you think it'd burn up inside the brown dwarf? It's a quantum warp in space! The dwarf only swallowed it because its orbital motion intersected with it. So…"

At last, Vivek figured it out. "So we just needed to hold back and wait until the Hubpoint came out the other side. I'm an idiot."

"You're impatient. Too hungry for the quick score. You need to learn to think first."

He gestured at the display wall. "Does that sort of situation happen often?"

"Nahh," said Nashira. "More likely you'll come out of a Hubpoint parsecs away from the dwarf… or one right in the middle of it. Most bad dives, you'll never know what killed you."

"Then why all this survival training?"

She smirked. "It encourages a healthy sense of denial."

The dark-skinned young man shook his head as he and Nashira left the ship. "It's insane that in sixteen thousand years, nobody's found a way to predict where a new Hub vector would come out, so we wouldn't have to risk our lives testing every one. Didn't I hear you used to work with a human who had an angle on cracking the problem?"

Nashira laughed. "That's a cosmic overstatement. David LaMacchia's a naïve kid with an impossible dream. He thinks his sheer ignorance will let him hit on an idea no smart person would ever think of." She chuckled as they reached the Hub scouts' ready room. "He once tried to get me to re-dive a vector with the ship facing backward to see if the Hub would send us in the opposite direction."

Her words caught the attention of Jeqqun. The veteran Poviqq scout turned to stare at them with the echolocation membrane above his bovine snout. "And yet," Jeqqun said, "the Dosperhag took him seriously enough to try to eliminate him. Twice."

"And me along with him!" Nashira pointed out. Turning back to Vivek, she said, "The Dospers are just paranoid. They got rich off having the one and only means of faster-than-light travel in their space, so even an imaginary threat to their monopoly gets their tentacles quivering."

"They're protecting our way of life," the long-limbed Poviqq protested. "Imagine the chaos if more Hubs could be manufactured. The warfare that would spread without a single nexus to regulate all interstellar travel. The crime. The illegal immigration. The shady travel agencies!"

"Nashira certainly knows about crime," said Evdrae. "You should hear her boast about her lawbreaking back on Earth."

"I don't 'boast,'" Nashira riposted. "I did what I had to do to make it out of that life."

The yellow-skinned Druagom scoffed. "And you're such a paragon of honesty now. Attempted claim fraud—"

"Those claims were rightfully mine! Well... the first one was."

"Smuggling bioweapons!"

"*Exposing* bioweapon smugglers. Just… slightly too late to stop them."

"And now you're openly associating with a crew of thieves and scoundrels."

"David got roped into their crew. I just keep him from hanging himself."

"You have an excuse for everything, don't you? But you still get to flout the rules with impunity because you're so special."

"Damn it, Evdrae, I've had to scrape and struggle to keep this job, just like the rest of you."

"Maybe before, under Vekredi. But ever since Rynyan took over, you can do no wrong. The advantage of sleeping with the boss."

"Oh, give it a rest!" Nashira groaned, though with less conviction than she could have mustered before two weeks ago. *It was only the one time.*

"Why else would he have taken the manager job?" Evdrae asked. "Sosyryn *never* take jobs."

At Vivek's questioning stare, Jeqqun explained: "They're so rich that they compete to *give* their wealth away. It's how they earn status." He sighed. "If I were Sosyryn, I'd be a much happier failure."

"But now Rynyan gets to lavish his favorite 'employee' with special treatment," Evdrae went on. "Upgrading her ship, indulging her absences… not to mention how many near-hits she's gotten lately, vectors almost in range of valuable finds. I don't know how, but Rynyan is skewing the assignments to improve Nashira's odds."

"Far be it from me to doubt that management is cheating us," Jeqqun countered. "But if they'd found a way to target Hub vectors, surely we'd all be out of work by now."

"Don't be so sure. If it were me, I'd offer it to the Dosperhag, buy my way out of this dead-end career. I'm sure they'd pay a fortune to keep it covered up."

"Then why hasn't Nashira quit already?"

"No need, when Rynyan will give her whatever she wants…

in trade for whatever *he* wants."

Nashira resisted the impulse to refute Evdrae's charge—at least until she and Vivek headed off to the food court for dinner. "The nerve of that jaundiced salamander! The idea that I have some special privilege is ridiculous. I've fought for everything I have, and I've never asked for anything I haven't earned."

"Good for you," Vivek said, patting her on the back. "As long as you remember that, it doesn't matter what anyone else thinks of you."

"Watch the hands, mate."

He pulled away, hands held wide. "Just being friendly. Don't worry, I remember what you said. Strictly professional."

"Good." She turned away to hide her expression. Vivek was certainly quite handsome, with a youthful drive and enthusiasm that reminded her of a more intense version of David LaMacchia. But the reminder was unwelcome. David may have been a foolish kid, but he was the kindest and most trustworthy person in her life, and he made her feel good about herself in a way nobody else ever had. Yet Nashira's jealousy had harmed their friendship, prompting the drunken self-loathing that had driven her to seduce Rynyan, leading to one night of sheer joy and fulfillment that Rynyan had made it humiliatingly clear she would never know again. Fearing she could no longer be satisfied by a partner without twin prehensile genitalia, and embarrassed by the melodrama her life had become, Nashira had resolved to swear off dating. Until further notice, her sexual gratification would be solely in her own hands.

The complication was, she liked Vivek. He had David's enthusiasm without his childishness. He was raw and impulsive, needing guidance as much as David had, but he was more practical and readier to learn. That was why she had volunteered to train him as Mansura's replacement, surprising even herself.

Still, she might not be around to mentor him much longer if her secret weapon paid off. Better, then, not to risk getting too close.

"But we are friends, right?" he asked her as they sat down to eat a few minutes later.

She focused on unwrapping her sandwich. "Ahh… sure. Friends. I guess."

"So if you did have some special edge for finding good Hub vectors, you'd cut me in on the action?"

Nashira laughed a bit too loudly. "Reckon, mate. If I ever find a magic crystal ball, you'll be the first to know. Hub scout's honor."

He chuckled—then grimaced at his first bite of the Pibnai curry he'd ordered. "They call this extra-spicy? I've drunk water with more bite!"

"I warned you. A proper hot curry would kill a Pibnai in one bite."

"Then I'd better go convince that vendor I have a death wish. Be right back."

Nashira picked at her fruit cup for a few moments before a familiar voice interrupted her. "Hi, Nashira. Can we talk?"

She sighed. "David. Look, this isn't the best time."

The sandy-haired American looked at her sadly. "It never is for you lately. That's why Rynyan sent me. You've been avoiding, well, both of us, and he figured you'd be more receptive to me." He smiled faintly. "I think he's finally catching on that you don't like him flirting with you."

Nashira almost laughed. "Er, yeah, we… worked that out a couple of weeks ago."

David's brow furrowed. "Then if it's not him, is it me? I know things got weird between us over Julio, but I want you know, there are no hard feelings."

She stared at him. "'No hard feelings?' Like it's that easy to fix everything."

He held her gaze patiently. "No, it isn't. But it's a good place to start."

Nashira fidgeted. Why couldn't he get angry with her like she deserved? "Look, we can talk about it later."

"When?" he pressed. "Nashira, we're worried about you. You've gotten so obsessed with your secret ancient vector list lately."

She panicked, looking around furtively. "Could you be quiet about that?"

"No, I will not be quiet. It's partly because of me that you found that list, and that Rynyan agreed to let you and Tsshar keep it secret. So I feel responsible for what's happening with you."

"Right, but let's not talk here. Sometime soon—"

"I know, I know. Sometime soon you'll dive on one of those ancient vectors and find a world that's still habitable and hasn't drifted too far off its Hubpoint. Or you'll discover some amazing technology left by the lost civilization before the Network."

"David—"

"It's only a matter of time, right? The list is your secret weapon, your guarantee that you'll strike it rich and get out of the scouting life. But that hasn't been working out so well, has it?"

"David, shut up!"

"I don't mean to be harsh, Nashira. I'm just worried that you're losing perspective. It's still Tsshar's list, you know. Even if she technically stole it from the pre-Network archive."

"Seriously, did you come down with an exposition virus?"

"She may tolerate you keeping it on the *Entropy*, but that doesn't mean—"

"Right, that's it!" She shot to her feet. "I told you, this is not the time!"

"Is this man bothering you, Nashira?"

She whirled at Vivek's voice, dreading what he might have overheard. Once his training was over, he'd be just another competitor like all the other scouts. She wasn't about to trust him with the truth about the crystal prism and its thousands of pre-Network dive coordinates—let alone split the profits once a vector finally paid off. If David's sudden bout of logorrhea had spoiled her secret...

"Ahh, no, it's nothing to concern you. Vivek, this is David LaMacchia."

David grinned. "Oh, you're Nashira's new trainee! I'm pleased to meet you." He shook the other man's hand. "I'm glad to see Nashira's made a new friend. And trust me, she's a terrific mentor. You're in great hands. Just..." He threw Nashira a sidelong look. "Make the most of it while you can."

The American went on his way, and the Indian resumed his seat. "You sure that was nothing you want to tell me about?"

She looked down. "Minor personal matter. Nothing that affects you."

Vivek nodded, giving no sign that he recognized her lie. Nashira relaxed and resumed their small talk. They had a nice, casual thing going, and she was happy to enjoy that while it lasted, free of any complications involving the vector list.

"He *stole* the vector list?!"

Rynyan Zynara ad Surynyyyyy'a paced the floor of the Hubstation's central office, dismayed by Nashira's sheepish admission. "This is bad. If word gets out that I knew of a discovery that could benefit the whole Network and kept it secret on behalf of just two people... why, my already-tarnished charitable reputation would never recover!"

The Sosyryn was the only other person in the room whose agitation came close to Nashira's own. David kept his own counsel, but his eyes betrayed a measure of relief that the list was gone. Next to him, Tsshar Murieff twitched her whiskerlike tendrils in amusement. "He steals it from your own ship," said the tiger-striped Mrwadj captain. "I like this little human. Maybe I make a deal with him instead."

Rynyan spun. "Do you think he'd agree to keep it quiet?"

"Of course he will," Nashira said. "He's a scout, isn't he? He'll see the advantage as readily as I did."

"You can't know that! Who can understand how humans think? Certainly not other humans, from what I've seen of you and David. Oh, Nashira, how could you let this happen?"

"How could *I*? The *puk gai* would never have found out if David here could keep his bloody gob shut!"

David stared. "It's not like you bothered to tell me you weren't alone!"

"We were in public!"

Tsshar leapt onto Rynyan's desk to get attention. "You all waste energy! He has the thing. We want the thing. We get the thing from him. That's how it works." As she spoke, a couple of her six monkeylike limbs absently rifled through the items on Rynyan's desk and pocketed a few, seemingly of their own volition. "He scouts for Rynyan, so Rynyan can find him, yes?"

"Certainly." Rynyan took his seat and worked the desk console. "I'm sure we can persuade him easily enough. A second scout would let us work through the list more efficiently."

"No way in hell!" Nashira cried. "I'm not gonna reward him for stealing my one way out!"

"Ah," Rynyan said, staring at his desk display. "We have a larger problem than we realized. Vivek Dhawan is listed on the passenger manifest for a ship that left the Hubcomplex four hours ago... en route for Dosp."

Nashira gasped. "Oh, no. Vivek listened to Evdrae. He thinks he can sell the list to the Dospers for a fortune. He's not going to take his chances diving its vectors—he's going for the sure payoff."

"Do you think the Dosperhag will buy it?" David wondered.

"They'd certainly be glad to promote the archaeological find," Rynyan said, "as well as any viable new vectors it might produce. The more of the Hub Network's bounty they can take credit for, the happier they are."

"Assuming they don't just arrange a fatal accident and bury the secret along with him," Nashira said with some relish.

"He's a clever thief," Tsshar replied. "He hides it, doesn't tell them where until his riches and safety are assured."

"Then we're screwed," Nashira said. "Dosp is two days' flight by passenger liner. The *Entropy* could beat him there with boosters, but installing them would take too long."

"Not necessarily," Rynyan said. "The Dosperhag are a fragile people, you know; they're not comfortable unless offworld visitors are closely regulated. For a novice Network member like a human to get through their bureaucracy would take days. He may claim to have something of value, but he'd have to wait for someone to get around to assessing that claim."

Nashira grinned. "But a Sosyryn could get premium access with no questions asked."

"Normally, of course. But my own standing with the Dosperhag has been... tenuous since I failed to deliver their spy's report on David's Hub research. And none of you would have any hope of penetrating the bureaucracy."

Nashira's grin was a distant memory. "Then we really are royally rooted."

Rynyan sighed. "It would be simple enough to disguise ourselves with a body swap... but no, that would never work."

David frowned. "Body swap?"

"Oh, yes," Rynyan replied. "It was quite the fad a couple of centuries ago. It's the same bioprinter technology used for limb and organ replacement and rejuvenation treatments. But it's also used for extreme body modifications, up to and including remaking yourself as an entirely different species, at least externally. You still have all the vital organs and cellular chemistry you need, but from the outside, you can become just about anything of the same rough structure."

David beamed. "That's amazing!"

"Yes, and quite fun. It's how I developed my love of cross-species sex. Back when it was fashionable, a few of my lovers and I liked to try on various forms and experiment with the possibilities."

Nashira was nodding now. "So we could disguise ourselves as higher-status species and gain a few bureaucratic laps on Vivek."

"But it wouldn't work. All full-body bioprinters are required to encode security features so that your true identity shows up on any scan. It's to prevent just the kind of fraud we're talking about. Why, before the security tags were mandated, impersonations were rampant. There was once a Heurhot actress so admired that she had ninety-seven impostors at the same time, a number of whom turned out to be better performers than her. Come award season, she swept the nominations in every acting category, and they couldn't figure out which ones of her to give the trophies to."

Tsshar clambered up the stem of Rynyan's antique torchiere lamp. "Bioprinters *in the Network* have security," she purred. "But we have an archive of toys from before the Network. My crew finds a bioprinter there just as good. Better. And no security codes. I already think of ways to use it. This Dosp caper is a good test run."

"Wait," Nashira said. "The archive just happens to have exactly the technology we need? That's a hell of a coincidence, isn't it?"

"Archive just happens to have many useful techs," Tsshar said, hanging from the lampshade. "It has the list too, remember? And many more things besides, which I save for when I need them."

"I never question a useful coincidence," Rynyan said. "Let's get this adventure underway, shall we? Oh, I wonder what species I want to be this time…"

"Hold on," David said. "Isn't this something we should think about first?"

"What's the matter?" Nashira asked. "I thought you loved trying new things."

"I do. The idea of experiencing life as another species is exciting. But what happens if we're caught? And what are we planning to do to Vivek if we catch him first?"

"If Vivek's out for profit, he should be easy enough to bribe," Rynyan said. "And if we're caught—why, the Dosperhag wouldn't dare harm a personage of my stature, so I could protect the rest of you."

"They tried to kill you twice, along with David and me," Nashira reminded him.

"In ways that would have looked like routine disappearances diving untried vectors. If anything happened to me on Dosp, it would bring far too much scrutiny."

"But what would it do to humanity's reputation if we were caught doing something criminal?" David asked. "The bioweapon thing was bad enough, but at least people saw us as victims there." He shook his head. "The whole reason I came to the Hub was to try to do something positive for humanity. We just keep drifting farther away from that."

"This isn't about humanity," Nashira told him. "Vivek stole from your friends. Your crewmates. *Me.* If he sells the Dospers that list, we lose our chance at changing our lives for the better. And the Dospers, the people who've been out to get us for months, get rewarded for playing dirty again. So what matters to you more, David? Humanity or your friends?"

After a moment's thought, David squared his shoulders. "Okay. I'm in. For my friends."

"You know," Rynyan mused, "it serves humanity better if Nashira scores a find from the list than if the Dosperhag do, so really, it's a false dichotomy."

Nashira glared. "Don't step on our moment."

12

"Are we sure this is safe?" David's question echoed off the walls of the cargo hold, which was mostly filled by the ancient bioprinter whose alien contours he studied. With little time to waste, Rynyan had hired a compact private courier even faster (and much more luxurious) than Nashira's Hubdiver, and they'd loaded the bioprinter aboard so they could undergo the hours-long metamorphosis en route. The courier could thrust hard enough to reach nearly half lightspeed in a matter of hours (with nanofog damping to protect the occupants from the acceleration), greatly improving their chances of intercepting Vivek in time. Taking a private ship would also give them time to practice with their new bodies and personas before trying to interact with other people.

"I mean, this thing is from an unknown civilization," David elaborated. "Plus, it's two hundred thousand years old. Does it even still work?" Nashira thought it was one of the more reasonable questions that had ever come from David's mouth.

Julio Rodriguez laughed and clapped the smaller man's shoulder with a big, beefy hand. "Don't worry about it," the dreadlocked engineer said. "It's self-regenerating technology, the same kind that kept the archive's systems running for so long. And it was preserved as well as anything else in the archive. I already tested it myself."

David stared at his boyfriend in surprise. "You did? When?"

"Remember that Poviqq 'passenger' aboard *Miifu* last week? The one who kept flirting until you said you were flattered, but already spoken for?" He laughed. "That was me. And

I do appreciate your loyalty." His tone was light, but Nashira did not miss the warning glare Julio sent her way.

Not that she had any interest in coming between him and David again; the latter had made his choice clear, and Nashira knew better than to chase an unattainable goal. Even though that was basically her job description.

"A Poviqq?" David asked, impressed. "All arms and legs, that stout barrel body? How did you fit all of… you… inside that?"

Tsshar's medical officer, a gray-striped Mrwadj female named Grriassh, fielded the question. "This replaces all but the most needed organs. It reconfigures the rest to fit the new shape or size."

"Essentially everything's negotiable except the brain," Julio summarized. "It's really quite an experience. Seeing through different eyes—or different sense organs altogether. Inhabiting a different shape, learning to move a whole new way. Mind and body aren't as separate as humans pretend—being in a different body changes your behavior, your emotions, in ways you can't predict. And it's more than the body. Identity is just as much about how the world sees us, reacts to us. Being seen so differently changed the way I saw myself."

David nodded. "That Poviqq was quieter than you. Not as bold or confident. I never would've guessed it was you."

"Well, it's hard to be as confident without all this." Julio gestured theatrically at his big, muscular frame, a body he took justifiable pride in. "But I'm going for something more powerful this time."

"You didn't have to come along," David told him.

"I wasn't going to let my boyfriend infiltrate the Dosperhag bureaucracy without protection. I'm going to take care of you, my love, and I'm going to do it as the most badass bipedal species available."

"Thank you." David kissed him warmly. "Me, I'm gonna be a Sosyryn. That's the only high-status species I've really spent any time with, thanks to Rynyan."

"An excellent choice," said Rynyan as he came around from the other side of the machine. "I can think of few better role models than myself. And you'll love being a Sosyryn. Everyone admires us so."

"So what are you going to be?" Nashira asked him.

"Ah-ah, that's my little surprise. But I know you'll love it!"

Nashira doubted that. After her tryst with Rynyan, it was Sosyryn anatomy and abilities that held the most interest for her. Following David's lead and becoming a Sosyryn herself might open some doors there—if not with Rynyan, then perhaps with some other Sosyryn she might meet on Dosp.

Am I being pathetic? she wondered. She had little enough trouble attracting men that she'd always considered it beneath her to chase them. But that was why she'd missed her shot with David. And she was about to become a member of the most spoiled, entitled species in the greater galaxy. Why not take advantage of that and just go after what she wanted?

"All right, we're ready," Julio said after a few more moments. "I've programmed each of the pods for the species we chose, and you can customize the parameters with the interface." He directed them to their respective pods. Once they had finished entering their specifications, he asked, "All set? Good. Grriassh will monitor, and once we're done, we'll reset the pods for her and Tsshar. Any more questions?" Met only with silence, Julio said, "Then let's do this." He began to strip.

David looked around as the others followed suit—or rather, followed unsuit. "Do we have to take off everything?"

"Oh, don't be such an Earthling," Nashira chided as she efficiently got her kit off. "It's nothing we haven't all seen before anyway."

"Okay." David began to disrobe gingerly, then paused. "Hold on—when did you and Rynyan see each other naked?"

Nashira hoped she wasn't blushing all over. "Just shut up and get in the pod."

Once the sedative wore off and Nashira took stock of herself, she feared for a moment that the transformation hadn't worked. Her body felt unchanged. "Did something go wrong?" she murmured—and was startled to hear the words emerge in a slurred version of Dyryna, the Sosyryn's primary language. *I don't speak Dyryna!* "What's going on?" More Dyryna—with sibilants and trills her own vocal tract could never produce.

Looking down at herself made her head reel. She could feel her own familiar body from the inside, but what she saw was massively different—taller and sleeker, the joints in odd proportions. The skin was darker and more golden than her own, like the color saturation had been turned up, though the downy fuzz that covered most of it was black. The breasts were flatter, more conical, higher and wider on the chest. And what she could glimpse of the pubic region was... complex. She definitely was not in a human body anymore. "Why do I—" Stopping herself, she enunciated more carefully. "Why do I still feel like me?" This time, it came out in Cantonese, as filtered through a Sosyryn mouth and larynx. She'd been trying for English.

Doctor Grriassh appeared in her view. The Mrwadj physician looked different somehow, her coloring more vivid, her details sharper. Nashira's perspective seemed to shift in odd ways as she moved her head and eyes to take in the sight. "Don't fight it," Grriassh said. "Your brain and neural system map the new perceptions to their standards. Like a phantom limb. The printed neural system includes hardwired interpreter protocols. It adapts between your senses and reflexes and the body's. Let it happen automatically."

At Grriassh's prompting, Nashira carefully climbed out of the pod. She stumbled at first, but the doctor's advice not to think too much about her movements proved sound. It took the neural software a few moments to calibrate, but soon she was walking fairly comfortably (by the flexible standards of a hard partier like herself), enough to get a look at her new body in the full-length mirror Julio had had the foresight to provide.

And she was... stunning! Her body was taut and athletic, like her own but more so. Her feathery mane was thick and full-bodied, its hue as lustrously black as her human hair—and she'd never quite realized what a gorgeous color that was until this moment. Even the sound of it rustling as she turned her head was sensual. Her eyes were big and wide-set, bright green instead of dark brown, and her face suggested the aspect of a panthress. Enjoying the sight of herself, she began roving her hands up and down her body, discovering new sensations. *Oh, my,* she thought once her hands reached her lower regions. *That's something I'll have to explore once I get some alone time.*

"You look amazing!"

The words were in Dyryna, but it wasn't Rynyan's voice. A different Sosyryn male appeared behind her in the mirror—shorter than Rynyan, with pale skin, golden eyes, sandy brown feathers and down... and some very impressive equipment down below. "David! Looking fine yourself."

He strode forward, uncharacteristically at ease with his nudity and her open scrutiny thereof. "I do look fantastic, don't I? I feel amazing, too. My senses are so heightened. Everything looks and sounds and smells so wonderful. No wonder Rynyan's such a sybarite." He blinked. "I didn't even know I knew that word. For that matter, how do we even know what makes a Sosyryn sexy?"

"Are you joking? We've grown up exposed to Network culture. Sosyryn are one of the most admired, celebrated species in the greater galaxy, so their aesthetic standards—" She stopped herself. *"Aai?* When did I ever have anything nice to say about Sosyryn?"

"Why not? You are one now," David said, leaning closer and putting a hand on her lower back. "Might as well learn to enjoy it. Maybe we could even try enjoying each other," he said, his hand sliding further down.

"David!" she cried, though she felt more excitement than outrage. This body's senses really were heightened, including her awareness of his very enticing pheromones. "When did you get so bold? And why didn't you try it months ago?"

"Just getting into character," he purred. "This is how Rynyan acts, right?"

"Even he wasn't this physically forward with me."

"Maybe that's because you never led him on."

"Hmm, maybe." She leaned in closer.

"David!"

The voice was deep, loud, guttural, like a bear's roar. They jumped apart guiltily and spun to face the Mkubnir that Julio had become. A bear was a good comparison, if a bear were covered in bronze pangolin scales and shaped like a stubby-tailed Godzilla. Nashira wondered how much the printer had needed to augment Julio's organs to sustain his increased body mass.

David stepped over to Julio, acting more like his normal meek self. "Don't worry, Julio—I was just practicing my Sosyryn act. Man, you look... powerful."

"Well, keep that in mind the next time you play method actor." Julio threw a menacing glare Nashira's way, and she hoped he would take his own advice about not getting too much into character. Mkubnir were known for their intense pair-bonding and fierce mating competitions.

Still, in this body, even the thrill of fear felt exhilarating. Or maybe it wasn't the body. After all, she was a Sosyryn now. Who would dare harm her? The very idea was laughable.

Whoa, Nashira thought, reflecting on her years growing up as a Hong Kong refugee in Australia. *So that's what racial privilege feels like. No wonder David assumes humans are entitled to success.*

The thought reminded her that being Sosyryn could convey other privileges. So she perked up when her newly heightened hearing picked up Grriassh helping Rynyan out of his transforming pod. Pausing to preen her mane a bit, she slinked around toward the other side of the printer unit. "Oi, Rynzers! Come out and let me get a look at you, my lad!"

"With pleasure!" With the easy agility of an old hand at body-swapping, Rynyan jumped into view, arms spread theatrically. "Isn't it just amazing?"

Nashira stared, unbelieving. The sight of a Pajhduh was not uncommon in the Network. They were one of the oldest known civilizations, prominent in politics and business. Nashira was accustomed to seeing their huge-eyed, loris-like faces, their backswept ceratopsian crests, their kangaroo legs and equine tails.

But what she had a hard time believing was the single massive, pendulous udder that hung from Rynyan's chest, jiggling like a sack of water in response to his every bouncy movement.

"You're... you're *female?*" she finally got out.

"Surprise! I figured, as long as I was remaking my body, what better opportunity to experience the wonders of the female form from the inside? And the Pajhduh female form has always been one of my very favorites," he added, clutching his udder.

"And you wear it really well, Rynyan," David said, the newly Sosyryn male looking the erstwhile one over with a lusty grin.

Julio cuffed him on the side of the head. "Seriously? Him too?"

"'Her,' please, for the duration," Rynyan said.

Julio scoffed, which sounded terrifying from a Mkubnir. "Maybe you can rebuild bodies, but you can't change your gender identity with the flip of a switch."

"Oh, of course I'm still as magnificently male as ever in my psyche, where it counts. And I'm still oriented toward females—sorry, David. But I went to all the trouble to dress up in this body, so I might as well embrace the role."

Rynyan's idea of how a female acts? Nashira thought. The idea was disturbing enough to ease her disappointment about his choice of physical sex. She'd dallied with the occasional female partner when she'd been bored enough or wasted enough, but she would never be as effortlessly bisexual as David—or, despite recent events, as xenophilic as Rynyan. Even this new, easily aroused Sosyryn body hadn't changed that.

Still, she found it easier than usual to shrug it all off. Being Sosyryn would give her a wealth of other options.

Remember it's temporary, an inner voice of reason reminded her. *Nashira Wing, human, still needs to keep that list away from the Dospers, or she won't have much of a life to get back to. That's more important than indulging this body's urges.*

Her eyes drifted back over to David as he showed off his new physique to Julio. *Isn't it?*

13

Dosp was a small, metal-poor planet around a dim star, made important only by its accidental proximity to the Hub. Vivek Dhawan had not expected to be impressed. Still, he felt a twinge of awe despite himself as his passenger transport's destination finally came into view in its virtual ports. The entire planet was surrounded by a vast orbital ring, an enormous complex whose rotating cylindrical segments provided multiple gravity levels and environmental conditions to accommodate all the Hub Network species whose members came here to deal with the Dosperhag. Some translator-implant programmer with too much time to kill had chosen to render its name in English as the Corona of Mass Transaction.

Once he disembarked onto the Corona, Vivek was immersed in a crowd far more diversely bizarre than anything he'd seen at Hubstation 3742, which was designed for beings of broadly humanlike anatomy and chemistry. Even in this vast, cathedral-like wedge of the cylinder section, with dozens of tiers of balconies and skywalks visible in the open, tapering space overhead, the ground level was as tightly packed and bustling as the busiest airports back home in India. The lines were just as long too, and just as slow.

Of course, there were no Dosperhag on this level, with its roughly Earthlike gravity. But if he strained his eyes, Vivek was fairly sure he could see some of the fragile cephalopods far overhead, using their tentacles to brachiate along the lattices of the upper levels. That was where Vivek needed to reach in order to offer them his priceless discovery.

All right, so he'd stolen his "discovery" from Nashira Wing, but so what? She'd obtained it from another thief, so she had no more claim than he did. Not to mention that she'd wasted her opportunity, passing up the surefire profit of selling the vector list to the Dospers just because she took a couple of murder attempts personally. Most of all, she'd lied to him—promising to share just such a secret even while she'd knowingly kept it from him. The selfish bitch deserved to be taken advantage of for that. Now she would be stuck in her dead-end job for the rest of her, possibly quite brief, life while he avoided that foolish risk and made his big score in record time. She would certainly know he'd stolen the list, but she couldn't admit she'd been working with criminals, not when the Dospers already considered her an enemy. There would be no way she could stop him now.

The thought kept Vivek from growing impatient as he waited in the long line for the registration desk, where visitors checked in and were directed to their destinations. The wait was long, but with no fear of pursuit, it was a luxury he could afford. Surely matters would be expedited once he explained why he was here.

Finally he reached the desk, and a blue-furred, rodent-featured K'slien clerk took down his name and Hubstation, then stamped his palm with a luminescent ink mark strobing in an animated pattern. "Follow the indicator to the waiting station for thirty-seven forty-two."

"Waiting station? Look, I have something important to offer the Dosperhag. If you'll just notify someone higher in authority—"

"Higher authorities can be contacted through the waiting station. You shall be called on at the earliest available opportunity. Thank you."

Aware that the Mkubnir behind him was getting annoyed, Vivek surrendered and moved on. If the authorities he wished to talk to were at the waiting station, then there was no point wasting further time on this mindless drone.

Following the animated glyph on his hand led Vivek to a passenger tram that carried him into what seemed like a small city of numbered waiting lounges, laid out like the gates of an airline terminal on a far larger scale. As he watched the

numbers outside gradually increase toward 3742, he eventually noticed the display screens positioned at the lounge entrances. They went by fast, but eventually his translator implant kicked in to interpret the text:
Now Serving 2816.
Vivek sighed. This was going to be a long wait.

Before they came too near the Dosp system, Tsshar instructed the others to place the bioprinter in a stealth pod and jettison it, so that security sweeps would not detect it onboard when they reached Dosp. "Don't we need it to change back?" an alarmed David asked.

"Don't worry," Julio replied. "We do this all the time to avoid inspections. Trajectories in vacuum are predictable things—it's how astronomers can launch probes and know exactly where they'll end up years later. And this mission will take a few days at most. Nobody else will know where to look for it in the vastness of space, but we can find it again whenever we want."

Rynyan and Tsshar had arranged a set of forged identities that should pass muster even with Dosperhag security, but practicing their new roles with only each other for company wasn't easy. Julio had no Mkubnir on hand to advise him, and though Nashira and Rynyan offered what pointers they could from their own encounters with the race, it was hard to know how much of his assumed behavior was authentic and how much was caricature. It helped that others would likely be too intimidated to question any eccentricities.

Tsshar and Grriassh had both sacrificed their lower pair of arms to become K'slien—diminutive arboreal mammals with a proclivity for operations and administration, ubiquitous and invisible enough in the higher echelons of power to be an ideal form for gaining high-level access. They took to their new personas effortlessly, as if they'd been practicing a scheme like this for some time—which they probably had.

David and Nashira should have had the advantage of Rynyan's advice on playing Sosyryn, but Rynyan was too busy playing around with his own new form (Nashira insisted on the pronoun, for his sex change was superficial and temporary).

While the rest of the team had been preparing for the mission, Rynyan had apparently spent his last few hours in the Hubcomplex buying a large quantity of Pajhduh lingerie—all designed to highlight and adorn an extra-large udder—which he was systematically modeling for himself in the mirror during the practice period. "It all looks great, Ryn—uh, Hruhnjihn," said David, who'd been cheerfully watching the show, on the theory that it was what Rynyan would do. "But I doubt you'll have much opportunity to show it off on the mission. You're supposed to be an administrator."

"That's 'Dame Sanafh' to you, Mister Lymasa." For practice, they were trying to use each other's assumed names as often as possible. "And for your information, the Pajhduh udder is esteemed as a symbol of a wise and dignified people. Showing it off will earn me respect. The same as when human females display their intermammary fossae to make males bow to their every wish."

"Yeah, not quite the same, Dame," Nashira put in, rolling her borrowed eyes.

"Anyway, as long as I carry the assets of a Pajhduh female, I intend to *milk* them for all they're worth." He chuckled as he leaned forward to show off the udder. "You see what I did there, Zyvyz?"

"It's hard to miss," David replied with a leer. "Still, it's not like you'll need all that lingerie once you're back to your own self."

Rynyan tilted his crested head back with pride. "You don't know that."

Nashira was grateful when they drew closer to Dosp's primary star, for her duties as a pilot distracted her from the others' interplay. To save time, Nashira opted to pass as close to the star as the ship's thermal regulators could handle. Soon, they were near enough to see the shimmering, mesh-like halo that surrounded the orange dwarf. "What is that, Julio—umm, Ghuiru?" David asked.

"It's their starlifting array, Zyvyz," Julio explained, keeping one massive, scaled arm wrapped around David's slender shoulders. "Tens of thousands of huge magnetic generators. The

Dosperhag commissioned them not long after they established the Network. They drew an immense, continuous flare out of the star, basically turning it into a rocket that dragged its planets along gravitationally. It's how they relocated their system to put the Hub within its outskirts." The technical explanation sounded incongruous in "Ghuiru Idroknel's" ursine growl.

"But that was nearly sixteen thousand years ago," David said. "I thought my mom was slow to take down the Christmas lights."

"They keep it for course correction," Nashira said. "The star needs the occasional nudge to cancel out perturbations from other passing stars—and you know how close those are packed hereabouts." She gestured at the display wall. Even with Dosp's primary filling much of the view, the dazzlingly dense starscape of the Central Bulge was still faintly visible in the background, a near-solid yellow glow filling half the sky.

"Plus," added Julio, "the controlled flares shave off a bit of the star's mass. That makes its core burn a bit cooler, increasing the life expectancy before the star swells into a red giant."

David stared. "But... that's billions of years from now."

"That's the Dospers for you," Nashira told him. "Afraid of every conceivable threat, no matter how remote. Like you figuring out the key to the Hub, Zyvyz."

The other human-turned-Sosyryn smirked. "Come to think of it, Nysyra, that is one heck of a long shot." Nashira had gotten off easy in the alias department. "Like a mere human could ever figure that out."

She stared. "Whatever happened to all that rubbish about the indomitable human spirit?"

"Spirit is one thing, ability another. Now that I'm not looking through human eyes, some things seem clearer."

A warning tone sounded, and a K'slien face appeared on the display wall. "Attention, incoming courier. Your approach vector is drawing too near our starlifting array. Please divert to the recommended trajectory, or defensive measures will be taken." The corrected course vector appeared below the turquoise-furred visage.

"Better do as he says, Nysyra," Julio advised. "It'd be easy enough for the array to throw a flare at *us*. That's the other reason they keep the thing around—the ultimate planetary defense for the ultimate paranoids."

"We're on the clock, remember, Ghuiru?" replied Nashira. "I got this."

Opening a return channel, she addressed the traffic controller in the haughtiest, most Rynyan-like tone she could manage. "No worries, mate. My name's Nysyra Vynyn, and my friends and I are on a charitable mission on behalf of Rysos." She hadn't practiced "Nysyra"'s clan name enough to risk trying to pronounce it. "And it's kind of urgent, so if you'll just let us go on our way, it'll be very much in your best interest, if you know what I mean."

After the few seconds it took for the lightspeed signal to make the round trip, one pair of the controller's eyes widened while the other blinked rapidly. "Oh, my apologies, Mistress Vynyn! I didn't realize we were being graced by Sosyryn visitors. Certainly any... benefits you wish to provide to our operations here will be of great benefit—no, sorry, I already said 'benefit'—ah, to the entire Hub Network."

"Still... you must understand, my employers are extremely strict about the safety of the array, so if you could see your way clear to modifying your course just slightly, it would be greatly appreciated. Surely one as charitable as yourself would not wish to see me disciplined or demoted."

"Did you not get that we're in a hurry? You wouldn't want me to be ungrateful, would you?"

"And would your... gratitude... cover any losses I might sustain for looking the other way?"

"Like I said, don't worry about it. It's all good."

The primate sighed in a mix of relief and resignation. "Very well. The... amended information is coming on your display now. Safe travels." The K'slien disappeared, and a new set of numbers lit up on the display wall—the routing information for the controller's bank account.

Nashira grinned at David. "See? I said I'd handle it."

Rynyan bounced over to them and planted his hands on his well-muscled hips. "Aren't you forgetting something, Nysyra?

You promised him a bribe."

"I didn't promise a bloody thing. I can't help it if he jumped to certain conclusions."

"Nysyra, he could lose his job! You owe him compensation for the risk he's taking."

"The Network has universal basic income. He won't starve."

Rynyan looked scandalized. "Being Sosyryn is a privilege, my friend, but it is also a grave responsibility. I can't have you damaging the Network's trust in the sincerity of our pledges."

"Fine. Bribe him out of your own hoard. I'm not giving up any of mine if I don't have to."

"Whatever you give away will be replenished, and then some. That's what it's for!"

"For you, maybe. I learned long ago never to give up anything that was mine. Hell, that's why we're here! And don't you forget it."

The lingerie-clad alien with the kangaroo legs and the single enormous boob gave her a solemn, disapproving look. Somehow, it fell rather short of the desired effect.

"Your reason for seeking an audience with the Dosperhag?" asked the spindly blue-gray Jiodeyn across the desk.

Vivek leaned forward eagerly. "I'm in possession of an artifact they will find very valuable. A list of thousands of unknown Hub vectors that—"

"I see. So your purpose is commercial?"

"No, you don't understand. This list could lead to the discovery of new planets, ancient artifacts—"

"Then your purpose is to request research funding."

"No, that's not it! I have the list. It's hidden somewhere safe, but I'm here to negotiate terms for handing it over. If you like, I can provide a sample of addresses to prove—"

"Then I shall put you down for 'commercial' after all. You say this is transportation-related?"

"Yes! I told you already!"

The longer he waited, the more Vivek questioned his earlier assurance that Nashira could do nothing to stop him. What about the Mrwadj captain from whom she'd obtained the list, or the Sosyryn station manager she'd unconvincingly denied sleeping with? Vivek had no idea what resources they could bring to bear. Maybe he was being paranoid, but he grew more eager by the hour to get this deal over with so he didn't have to worry about who was coming up behind him.

"Now: are you representing yourself or a larger agency or firm?"

Vivek seethed. "Look, I'm under some time pressure here. Is there someone else I could talk to?"

"Certainly, sir, that's why we're here. Just a few more questions, and I'll be able to forward your application to speak to a representative."

Vivek was stunned. "You mean... you're not the representative?"

"I'm the application agent. I'm here to facilitate your entry into the next tier of the Corona. To that end, if you'll just bear with me for a few more questions, I'll put your application right in, and with luck, you should receive a reply within fifteen hours."

"*Fifteen—*" He caught himself. No sense getting thrown out for trying to strangle an application agent. "Okay. So once I get to the next tier, then I'll be able to talk to a Dosperhag?"

The Jiodeyn chuckled. "Why, no, sir. The representative will hear your petition and decide whether it warrants forwarding to a higher tier."

"And how many tiers does it take to get to the Dospers?"

"I wouldn't know, sir. That's above my tier."

The human buried his face in his hands. "Of course it is."

"We're almost done, sir. Just a few more questions, and we'll soon have you tiering up."

Vivek suppressed a sob. "Sooner than you think!"

Swapping into high-status species proved a mixed blessing once the disguised party disembarked onto the Corona of Mass Transaction. The Dosperhag's insistence on a thorough security sweep of every ship threatened to delay their entry, but David, already getting the hang of living as a Sosyryn, offered a liberal greasing of palms to expedite matters. The dock security staff was diligent, though, insisting that corners could not be cut where safety was concerned. Rynyan insisted on the importance of his party's mission, but with his skimpy attire and the way he flounced and flirted, putting on a horny male's fantasy of how a beautiful female should behave, Nashira doubted he could sell the air of Pajhduh authority he was going for. The security staffers merely stared, nonplussed.

But at least Rynyan's antics drew the crowd's attention, and Nashira could use that. Raising her chin and her voice, she spoke in the haughtiest Sosyryn tones she could manage. "Listen, mate. We're on an urgent charity mission here. Lives are at stake! Thousands—maybe millions of lives! Every minute you keep us waiting, more sick children will die! Really adorable sick children! Do you really want to be responsible for that? Do you want the galaxy to know you had a chance to help us save all those innocent, cute little lives, and you instead decided to show off how well you've memorized a rule book?"

It filled Nashira with satisfaction to see the humiliated security officers waive all but the most essential safety measures to hasten the party through. It was a heady feeling to be the one on top for a change. "I could get used to being a Sosyryn," Nashira purred once the group was past the checkpoint.

Rynyan glared, trying and failing to cross his arms over his massive teat. "I've never seen a Sosyryn use charity as a bludgeon. Especially as a cover for helping themselves."

"Oh, come off it. Charity's how you lot compete for status. It's always about helping yourselves."

"That status is earned through our actions, Nysyra. You don't want to create a scandal and lose your influence." He lowered his head. "Believe me, I know what that's like. Why do you think I was so eager to stop being me for a while?"

"Whatever. As long as my influence lasts long enough to get my hands around Vivek's throat."

Once within the Corona proper, the group had to split up, for the admissions process was organized by Hubstation. Sosyryn and Pajhduh were both served by Hubstation 9, so David and Nashira were able to stay with Rynyan, but Julio and the Mrwadj had to go their separate ways. This was to their advantage, for they could follow several lines of investigation that way. Julio would use his Mkubnir persona to connect with Corona security, while Tsshar and Grriassh would blend in with the administrative staff and hack the data systems. The humans and Rynyan, meanwhile, would use their new species' prestige and influence to seek what they needed.

This was more easily said than done, for the Corona's bureaucracy was vast and heavily partitioned. The employees of their intake station knew only their own localized responsibilities; at best, they could refer the group to higher-level bureaucrats who could tell them where to find the still-higher bureaucrats who could tell them what they wanted to know.

"This is bizarre," David said after he'd bribed a low-level functionary into letting them jump the queue to meet with the functionary on the next tier up. "Their jobs seem even more menial than ours. Why can't they just automate all this?"

"The Dosperhag mistrust sapient AIs," Rynyan said. "They're nervous enough around bigger and stronger species—imagine how they feel about more intelligent entities."

"Besides," Nashira said, "these poor sods *want* to be here. They don't have to work for a living, but they choose to be cogs in this machine so they can feel close to the center of power. It's pathetic. They're chasing something bigger and better, and just trapping themselves in smaller lives." She gestured toward the upper levels of the vast atrium they occupied, where her keen Sosyryn eyes could discern the slithering, skittering movements of the Dosperhag on their brachiating lattices, their multiple eyes aimed ever downward at the lower tiers. "Look at them up there. It's their primal instinct. Hiding in the branches, keeping an eye on the predators far below. They say the Corona facilitates interaction between Dosp and the rest of the Network, but it's really to prevent interaction. This whole space is designed to keep the rest of us penned and herded like cattle. They'll never let any of us climb to their level. Not even Sosyryn or Pajhduh."

Despite her words, the trio eventually found themselves in the office of a Corona staffer high-ranked enough to track down Vivek's location and authorize their passage. This official was a genuine Pajhduh female, her udder half the size of Rynyan's and significantly less exposed. "If you'd care to tell me what your interest in this human is, Dame Sahnafh?" she asked.

"I'm sorry, my dear," Rynyan replied in his most flirtatious tones, "but I'm afraid it's a very sensitive matter. You'll just have to take my word that it's nothing that could trouble the Dosperhag. As long as we reach Vivek Dhawan in time, they need never be aware of it at all." He leaned forward over the desk until his udder almost brushed against the official's. "So can I count on you to help a sister out? There could be... *ample* benefits in it for you."

Nashira winced. Surely a genuine Pajhduh female would see right through Rynyan's ridiculous drag act. At any moment, the official would have him arrested as an impostor or a lunatic.

"Why, certainly, Dame Sahnafh," the official said, staring at Rynyan's udder with a cowed expression. "I would never doubt the word of one of your... stature. I'll be happy to get you the information you need, and I assure you that your confidence will be respected."

Nashira could only stare dumbstruck as the official called up the data and obsequiously offered it to Rynyan. "What did I tell you?" the faux Pajhduh whispered to her as they left the real one's office. "A symbol worthy of respect."

14

Once the disguised trio reached the office to which Vivek had applied for a hearing, they found that his application had not yet cleared, so he was still one tier below. Rather than braving another layer of bureaucracy, Rynyan suggested that they speak to the office's administrator before Vivek arrived. But even with their Hubstation 9 status, they still had to wait behind a number of other petitioners. Nashira tried to browbeat the receptionist into expediting matters, but the staffers at this tier were unimpressed by her Sosyryn cachet. Rynyan pulled her back and suggested that she and David wait while he had a go.

"Thank you, Dame," Nashira heard the Ziovris receptionist murmur to Rynyan, evidently underestimating the acuity of her hearing. "Those Sosyryn, always expecting the rest of us to be happy to help them out. It's not like anyone actually *likes* them—we're just hoping they'll toss a little charity our way if we stroke their egos. But I don't have to tell you that, do I?" Rynyan just stared, then bounced dejectedly over to sulk in a corner.

But the receptionist's slur gave David an idea. He spent the next half-hour working the room, talking to the other petitioners to find out what they sought, making donations where he could to solve their problems on the spot, or dragging Rynyan out of the corner to offer Dame Sahnafh's connections and negotiating acumen where an influx of funds was not sufficient.

David encouraged Nashira to get in on the act as well. "This feels great—having all the resources I need to help other people. I'm even thinking, maybe this is a more practical way to help humanity than some wild goose chase to crack the Hub. I could donate so much to Earth before I change back."

"I thought you didn't want humans to be a charity case," Rynyan said.

"Well, I'm still human on the inside," David replied with a shrug. "So it'd still basically count as doing it ourselves."

That didn't sound like the David she knew, but Nashira shook it off. After all, he was sounding pragmatic for once. With access to Rysos's nigh-inexhaustible treasuries, there was no limit to what they could achieve. Why let principles forged in poverty stand in their way?

Besides, there were other things one could do with a bottomless Sosyryn bank account. While David continued his charitable rounds, Nashira imagined all the ways she could threaten to use Sosyryn clout to ruin Vivek's life if he didn't hand the list over—and all the ways she actually could ruin his life just for fun once he had.

The other reason she let David handle the schmoozing was because he was rather exciting to watch. Not only did he make a very fetching Sosyryn, but his new confidence and authority blended with his innate, open-minded enthusiasm to make him a very compelling presence. He dominated the room with his charm and self-assurance, flirting playfully with everyone regardless of species or sex. As Nashira watched him, she reflected on the unequalled pleasures of her one night with Rynyan. The idea of Sosyryn sexual prowess and confidence combined with David's warmth and kindness was overpowering, especially in the easily aroused body she now occupied.

In time, with the other petitioners thinned out, the trio was led into a private meeting lounge and asked to wait. They were still being herded and put off, but at least their new surroundings were comfortable, offering snacks, drinks, and other amenities. David and Nashira laughed together and flirted as they sampled the bar, but Rynyan was still sulking, barely noticing the building sexual tension.

Before long, Rynyan got a call from Julio, requesting his aid with some problem. "Can you handle things here?" he asked. "I'll try not to be long."

"Go ahead," David said as he fed Nashira a wedge of nectar-covered fruit. "We'll be fine here."

Nashira pounced on David before the door had even latched shut behind Rynyan. David tried to offer a token protest in those few moments when his lips were free, but the heady rush of their Sosyryn pheromones swiftly overwhelmed him, and soon he was tearing at her clothes as eagerly as she tore at his.

What followed was a torrent of sensations that Nashira could barely classify, as her brain-body interface strove to interpret Sosyryn sexual pleasures in terms a human brain could understand. But that very duality made the sensations doubly extraordinary—even hallucinatory. She'd had sex while tripping before, but the effects of one indulgence on the nervous system tended to interfere with those of the other. Her printed body's adaptive interface was designed to harmonize conflicting neural processes and sensory inputs, so that wasn't a problem here. She could feel her own human body as a phantom within her Sosyryn body, and both bodies were getting the rooting of their lives. It even felt as if, in some weird way, both her bodies were making love to each other from the inside. Nashira soon lost track of all sense of duration, all coherent thought, as the swirl of overlapping sensations engulfed her.

Until the claws of an enraged Mkubnir clamped down on her limbs and hurled her across the room.

"Oh, my," she distantly heard Rynyan's voice echoing from somewhere in the whirling centrifuge the suite had now become. "Good job, you two! I was only gone twenty minutes!"

But the other new arrival was not so impressed. Julio's massive digits closed around her neck and dragged her up the wall she'd struck. Even with Sosyryn height, her feet dangled. "Julio, don't hurt her!" David cried, clutching his boyfriend's arm. "I'm the one who messed up. I should never have let that happen."

"You just did what you thought Rynyan would do," Julio growled. "You were stupid, but not malicious—same as always. I can forgive that." His gaze sharpened on Nashira. "But *you*..."

"Really," Rynyan interposed, "does *everyone* have such a low opinion of Sosyryn? Why didn't anyone ever tell us?"

After a moment, Julio took a deep breath, visibly controlled

himself, and let Nashira go. Rynyan caught her arm before she fell. "I did," she told him hoarsely, "all the time."
"I thought that was flirting."
"You would."
"True. And to be fair to David, having sex with you is definitely in character for me. Although you were human when we did it, of course." Nashira winced, and David and Julio stared. "What? It was just the one time. It wasn't even that memorable."

Normally she would've punched him right in the udder, but she found her recent sexual choices indefensible. "I'm sorry too, Julio," she said. "I seduced him. It was stupid. But it's this damn alien body. I can't control its urges."

"It's not that you can't," Julio countered. "It's that you don't want to. Ever since you put on that skin, you've been abusing it. Using it to intimidate people, to bulldoze over them. Hoarding wealth that's meant to be given away. Even putting people's jobs at risk for your own convenience."

"I'm just fighting for what's mine! All my life, I've had to fight to get what I deserved and fight even harder to keep it. When people try to hold me down, I punch back!"

"Maybe," Julio said. "But *you're not punching upward anymore.*" His words brought her up short, and he continued. "These people you're fighting now—they're not the ones with privilege. You are. You don't need to struggle tooth and nail against them, because they're weaker than you. But you're still fighting them just as hard. And you know why? Because you don't fight to defend yourself. I know you did to start with, back on Earth—but not anymore. Now, you fight because you like it. You've become a bully, Nashira. And having power has brought out the worst in you."

There was nothing she could say to that—especially when she saw that David couldn't meet her eyes. All she could do was follow his lead by finding her clothes and getting dressed.

"Well, now that that's settled," Rynyan said with forced cheer, "I should mention why Julio wanted to see me. Apparently his questioning about Vivek got a bit too aggressive. Since he's Mkubnir, the Corona staff assumed it was a Hub security matter, and with the three of us simultaneously talking about how urgent it was, well, one thing led to another. Tsshar notified us that Vivek's been detained by Corona security. They're taking him up for interrogation now."

Nashira felt the room spin again. If the Dospers questioned Vivek, he'd surely give up the list rather than risk imprisonment. "That's it," she moaned. "We're done for."

"Not necessarily," Rynyan said. "As the parties who alerted them to the 'threat,' we've been invited to sit in on the interrogation. So we have one more chance to handle this… somehow."

The security center was on the highest tier the visitors had yet reached—high enough to be within plain sight of the Dosperhag-occupied tiers overhead. The soft-bodied, almost translucent cephalopods were still dozens of meters above, and in place of a ceiling, Nashira could see the haze of a security barrier, a dense field of nanofog that would congeal around anything that tried to penetrate it. Still, she felt more intensely scrutinized by the Dosperhag than ever before—especially once Rynyan pointed out to her that one of the principal Dosperhag observers watching them from the lowest tier was Morjepas, the one who'd been spying on her and David for months and almost gotten them killed twice. As the supervisor responsible for Hubstation 3742, he'd naturally been called in to consult when a scout from that Hubstation had been arrested. Nashira tried to reassure herself that there was no way Morjepas could recognize her as Nysyra Vynyn, but being under his direct gaze was unnerving nonetheless. Even though she was an invited guest, she felt more like a gladiator in a Roman arena.

She could only imagine how Vivek Dhawan felt. He sat in a lowered pit in the center of the room, only a meter or so down, but his hands were manacled to a plinth in its center while a Mkubnir even bigger and scarier than Julio sat across from him, with others bigger still flanking the edges of the pit along with Nashira's party of spectators. (Tsshar and Grriassh were absent; according to the captain's update over their comms, the two Mrwadj had successfully infiltrated the clerical staff and would remain there to run interference in case the group needed to make an escape. Nashira suspected they had some other agenda in mind, though; Mrwadj usually did.)

It felt good to Nashira to see the man who had betrayed her trust brought so low. But that satisfaction was tainted by Julio's recent words. She tried to shake it off. Maybe she'd gotten a little carried away with her newfound power, but if anyone deserved to suffer for her pleasure, it was Vivek Dhawan. She just hoped she'd find some way to let him know that she was the one responsible.

Still, they couldn't let Vivek be interrogated. If he gave up the vector list to the Dosperhag, they would assign all the top Hub scouts to test its addresses as swiftly as possible—and there was no chance that a human from a backwater Hubstation would be one of them. But Julio was trying to convince the Mkubnir officers that this was a misunderstanding over a minor personal matter and that Vivek should be released into their custody.

Still, the chief interrogator, Kmugnik, was not about to release Vivek purely on Julio's say-so. "You say this is a private matter," the genuine Mkubnir boomed. "Yet this human does not appear to recognize you."

"I don't," Vivek insisted from his seat opposite Kmugnik. "I swear, I've never seen any of them before. Listen, I'm no threat to the Network! I came here to sell you something that could help you!"

"Something you stole from these people?" the chief interrogator guessed.

"No! Something I... found. It's rightfully mine. I earned it!"

"Earned it?" Nashira couldn't help blurting out. "You spied on a private conversation and stole it from—" She stopped herself in time.

Vivek stared. "How could you know that? Who are you?"

Kmugnik smashed his arms down on the plinth, startling him. "Then you are a spy! Is your intention sabotage?"

"No! It's nothing like that. Okay, so I didn't exactly obtain it honestly—but neither did the woman I took it from! She was keeping it from you. I came here to give—well, sell it to you!"

"A human female?" Kmugnik consulted his data pad. "You are listed as a trainee of Hub scout Blue 662 Red 769, Nashira

Wing Wai-hing, alias Nashira Wing, alias Róng Huìqìng, alias Bringer-of-Good-News Airfoil."

Up in the gallery, Morjepas tensed, his tentacles writhing. Nashira didn't need to be fluent in Dosperhag body language to tell that he recognized her name and was not happy to hear it. She was starting to enjoy the sensation of standing right under his beak without him knowing it.

"Yes, that's her! You see, she was working with a Mrwadj captain who'd come into possession of—"

"The same Nashira Wing Wai-hing implicated as an accomplice in multiple disruptive acts over the past nine months, including the smuggling of the bioweapon used to render the Zeghryk species infertile."

Nashira controlled her shock. Among her fellow scouts, it had been easy to dismiss such charges as rumors. Knowing that they were part of her official reputation on Dosp made her want to stay in Sosyryn guise forever.

"Exactly. She's the one you should have in here, not me." Vivek chuckled. "Hell, if you have a problem with Wing, you should be grateful for the way I played her. I could tell she had a thing for the nice-guy routine. At first, I was just hoping to get her into bed, but I got an even better payoff out of it. If you can't handle her, maybe you need my help."

Nashira clenched her fists so hard that her tapered nails drew blood. She no longer knew which side she should be rooting against.

Kmugnik growled. "You humans. So arrogant in your inexperience, as new Network members so often are. So convinced your ignorance of your limitations makes you superior. You are nothing! Just one more drain on the charity of the Network. One more ignorant, warlike breed with nothing to offer but need and instability. You have no great physical or mental advantages, no exceptional resources, only a paltry few millennia of civilization and art. You will never catch up with the rest of us, let alone surpass us." He gestured upward. "In time, you will learn to accept your place and be grateful for what our Dosperhag benefactors have built for the benefit of all. I will take pleasure in teaching you that lesson, human spy."

He looked up at the spectators whom he beheld as two Sosyryn, a Pajhduh, and a fellow Mkubnir. "Or perhaps these people you have wronged would prefer to instruct you. These members of fine, upstanding civilizations who have earned more respect and appreciation than your infantile breed could earn for another ten thousand years. Just tell us his crimes," Kmugnik said to them, "and let us know what punishment you feel he deserves. *Your* word will carry the weight his will not."

The interrogator was giving Nashira the chance to obtain everything she wanted. She could tell a story that would inoculate the authorities against Vivek's claims, then arrange to get him alone and force him to talk. Being Nysyra Vynyn gave her power and license beyond what Nashira Wing had ever known.

But that thought made her remember what Nashira Wing had known. A life on Earth as a refugee, marginalized and degraded for her race, her sex, and her economic standing. A life in the Hubcomplex as a menial outsider, accepted only by the other menials who shared her station, and not very well liked by most of them.

Looking at the mix of defiance, fear, and frustration in Vivek Dhawan's eyes, she saw her younger self looking back—and she was ashamed of how she'd treated him as her trainee. He may have imagined he was playing her, but he had been the one in the weaker position, and she hadn't hesitated to lie to him. Was it any wonder he'd betrayed her right back? Julio was wrong; she'd been punching downward even before the body swap.

Granted, Vivek was no innocent soul like David. But taking Kmugnik's offer would mean endorsing everything David stood against. More—it would mean admitting that what the Network thought of *her* was true. At this moment, in a Sosyryn skin, she finally understood why David strove so hard on behalf of humanity.

But what do I strive for? Nashira asked herself. For nine years, she'd risked her life chasing that one great discovery that would get her out of Hub scouting and earn her a higher rank in the Network. Yet she'd seen the Corona staffers who chased an equivalent dream. Their desire to climb nearer the center of power had trapped them in lives even more menial than her own.

If the system itself was what trapped them, why had she ever thought that playing by the system's rules would set her free?

"He's telling the truth," Nashira said, to her own amazement. "About one thing, anyway. He only came here to sell you a list of good Hub vectors from an ancient pre-Network civilization. Old enough that the destinations have drifted off their Hubpoints by now... but if even a few percent out of tens of thousands are reachable, the boon to the Network could be vast."

She stepped down into the pit, holding Vivek's gaze. "But the truth is, he stole it from me." David, Rynyan, and Julio stared at her in shock—was she about to out them all? Giving them a slight nod, she went on: "My friends Ghuiru and Dame Sahnafh found that list on an archaeological dig that Zyvyz and I underwrote. Vivek was one of their laborers. He got greedy and stole the list before we could donate it to the Network. We pursued him so urgently because..." She chuckled. "Well, you know how it is. If someone else gave the list to the Network—and *earned* money from it—that would have cheated us out of a monumental boost to our donation tallies." Kmugnik and his associates nodded in understanding.

Nashira circled the plinth and put her hands on the shoulders of a very bewildered Vivek. "But we Sosyryn are nothing if not charitable. I don't blame Vivek for his impulsive act; after all, he is just a lowly human who doesn't understand how true civilization functions. And of course, the same goes for his partners David LaMacchia and *especially* Nashira Wing." She laughed. "They're nuisances, to be sure, but they're too petty and naïve to be actually harmful. And Wing is actually rather good at her job—well overdue for a bonus, I'd say. So, really, you should just stop bothering with any investigations or sanctions you might be considering against them. As a favor to me, and to the Sosyryn people, who've taken an interest in shepherding these poor, ignorant primitives along the slow uphill climb to enlightenment." As she spoke, she clapped Vivek's shoulders with amiable force.

Kmugnik tilted his heavy-scaled head upward to consult

with the Dosperhag, who conveyed their thoughts with flashes of chromatophoric color beneath their translucent skin. Morjepas, unsurprisingly, seemed hostile to her recommendation, but the other Dosper panelists argued him down, not wishing to dishonor a Sosyryn's heartfelt plea for charity. "Your eloquence and compassion are moving, Mistress Vynyn," Kmugnik finally said, interpreting their instructions. "We would expect no less from your wise and benevolent people. But Vivek Dhawan has confessed to an act of theft, and you have confirmed it. We cannot simply overlook that."

"No, of course the list must be returned," Nashira replied. "But surely you could agree to go easy on this poor, ignorant sod if..." She gritted her teeth and wrenched her eyes shut, her sharp nails digging deeper into Vivek's shoulders. "If he tells you all, right now, where he hid the vector list. Once your agents in the Hubcomplex retrieve it, why, an equitable balance will be restored, and you can remand Vivek into our custody for whatever discipline we see fit."

Vivek stared up at her, dawning realization in his eyes. Maybe he recognized something in her voice, or maybe it was her slang that tipped him off. He knew that she was Nashira Wing, though he had no idea how—or why she was helping him. But he recognized that she was giving him the only possible way out—and giving up her own ticket to success for his sake. "All right," he said, still holding her gaze with something like apology and gratitude. "I'll tell you where it is."

He started to describe the list's hiding place, and Nashira felt her dreams evaporate. But the respect and understanding in David's and Rynyan's eyes—and especially Julio's—outweighed her sense of loss.

15

"I still can't believe that's you inside that body," Vivek said to Nashira as the reunited group flew outward from Dosp in their rented ship. "Any more than I can believe you helped me. I promise, I won't waste this second chance. I'm a changed man from now on. I—"

"Oh, don't try to con me again," Nashira told him. "I helped you because we're the same. So don't think I don't see through you." She turned her gaze to David. "Maybe you really could come to your senses, Vivek... with the right person to help you. But it's not gonna be me. Once we're back at the Hubcomplex, you and I are done."

"And you'll have to find employment somewhere else," Rynyan added. "I expect a *little* scheming and cheating from my Hub scouts, but there are limits. Especially when it comes to hurting my friends."

Vivek sighed. "Well, it was fun while it lasted." His gaze shifted back to Nashira. "Though I wish I'd at least gotten you into bed. That's a dive I doubt any man will ever figure out how to make."

Nashira traded a look with Rynyan and David. The three of them broke out laughing, though David looked embarrassed. But after a moment, Julio laughed even louder, to both David's and Nashira's relief. Vivek, confused but sensing that they were laughing at his expense somehow, slunk away sullenly.

Taking Julio's good humor as encouragement, Nashira ventured, "You know, you don't have to worry about me and David anymore. I won't try that again. I mean, don't get me wrong, David—it was amazing. But it wasn't what I really wanted."

"Me neither," David said. "I mean, we weren't in our own bodies. Does that even count?"

Julio gave him a no-nonsense look. "It counts."

"No, that's not what I mean," Nashira said. She took a moment to build up her courage. "I thought... that I was in love with you. But I see now... that isn't really what I feel for you. I didn't realize that because... what I do feel is something I've never felt before. I've... never had a best friend before." She cleared her throat. "But that's what you are. And that's all I want from you anymore."

David's Sosyryn face lit up in a smile and he took her hand in both of his. "You have it," he said. "You're my best friend too."

She blinked convulsively. Could Sosyryn cry?

A small, furry body pounced onto Nashira from behind, making her stagger. Even in a K'slien frame, Tsshar was still all Mrwadj. "You and I need to talk, little Sosyryn-human," she said, her face hanging upside-down in front of Nashira's. "I admire the way you steal the list from me—it's a tactic I never anticipate. But you make it public, share with the Network. You give me no chance to steal it back. Hardly fair."

"Well, you're welcome to try stealing something else from me," Nashira countered. "Oh, that's right, I don't own anything of value. So sad."

"It's not like you were all that helpful," Rynyan told the captain. "You were off on your own the whole trip. What were you really doing all that time?"

"Oh, you like this. Especially my little David." Tsshar pushed off Nashira's shoulders, sending her reeling, and landed in David's lap. Nashira reflexively checked her pockets and found that Tsshar had made off with her credit rod again. "Grriassh and I hack into Corona data systems. Probe deepest darkest secrets of Hub. Research they want no one to know."

David perked up, amazed. "You mean... there actually *is* some secret they've been keeping about how the Hub works?"

"Yes!" Tsshar answered cheerily, dodging Nashira's attempts to retrieve her rod. "Hub is totally random! No pattern at all to where new vector comes out—can be anywhere, but first passage correlates vector with destination, makes it consistent afterward. But no one can ever predict where a new vector comes out. Good secret, yes?"

David looked stunned. Clinging to skepticism on his behalf, Nashira asked, "Wait a minute. Why would they even hide something like that? What's the big deal?"

"If vectors are random," Tsshar explained, "there's non-zero chance two vectors open on same point." She used both Nashira's credit rod and, apparently, David's as visual aids, bringing them together and making them both vanish with sleight of hand. "Collapse correlation. Dosperhag want no one to know their worlds could lose their Hubpoints."

"That's gotta be one chance in a trillion! Less!"

"Still not zero. Not forever sure. Dospers want no one to lose faith in the system." She chuckled. "I hold onto this. Maybe I find good way to blackmail Dospers." Tsshar straightened. "But not yet. Now we near rendezvous point with bioprinter pod. We can get back in our own lovely bodies."

She bounded forward to the cockpit, and Rynyan and Julio followed. David stayed where he was, and Nashira touched his shoulder. "Maybe... maybe the Dospers are wrong. You always said, maybe it took a new perspective to see through the accepted assumptions."

After a moment, David shrugged it off. "Maybe. Somehow, I'm not too upset about it. Probably just this Sosyryn cockiness. But it'll probably hit me hard once I'm human again." With a sigh, he rose and started to move forward.

"I don't know," Nashira said, taking his arm and strolling with him. "I bet that once you're David again instead of Zyvyz, you'll get back that lunatic optimism that comes from being an underdog. The Man of LaMacchia, always tilting at windmills."

"After all—the problem with being up too high is that you lose perspective on what's really important."

He smiled at her. "You know something, Nashira? You've never sounded so human."

She smiled back. "I never thought that would sound like a compliment from a Sosyryn mouth."

"Well, I can't wait to be back in my own body." He grinned.

"And especially for Julio to be back in his." Nashira laughed with him as they entered the cockpit.

"That may be harder than we thought," Julio rumbled, scanning the console in agitation. "We can't find the stealth pod."

"What?" Nashira cried. "How could it be off course? We're in open space!"

"Open space on the edge of the galactic core," Julio reminded her. "Unpredictable perturbations from passing stars, remember?"

"No trouble," Tsshar said. "It can't go far since we drop it off. Only few billion cubic kilometers to search."

"To find a pod you have to be within a kilometer of to spot!" Nashira cried. "We could be searching for months! Shit, what if a meteoroid hit it? We could be stuck in these bodies forever!"

"Rrr, no," Grriassh said. "Rush jobs. Not designed for long-term occupancy. Last a year at most."

"Are you kidding me?!"

"No problem. At worst, we use another bioprinter, get long-term bodies made. Just not our own," the Mrwadj doctor added sheepishly. "We never figure out how to back up printer's data. So we must approximate. Use generic forms, reconstruct specifics from videos, medical data."

"You mean settle for a cheap knockoff of my own body? To hell with that! I'm a custom job! I've spent thirty-three years breaking in that body, and I've got all the settings the way I like them!" Nashira pushed forward. "Let me at those sensors. Gotta be a way to boost them. Julio, start brainstorming! Science something up! Find me my real goddamn body before it gets away!"

"Well, it just goes to show," Rynyan mused. "Switching identities is all fun and games until somebody loses an I."

AFTERWORD: HUBBA HUBBA

Once *Hub Space: Tales from the Greater Galaxy* came out in 2015, collecting the first three Hub stories "The Hub of the Matter" (*Analog Science Fiction and Fact*, March 2010), "Home is Where the Hub Is" (*Analog*, December 2010), and "Make Hub, Not War" (*Analog*, November 2013), it gave me the impetus to begin working on further adventures for Nashira, David, and Rynan. I approached the project with an eye toward writing a whole trilogy of stories in quick succession, so I could promptly collect them once they were published—"writing for the trade," as they say in comics (referring to the tendency to plot and pace stories to suit their eventual trade-paperback collections rather than the individual monthly issues). I wanted to devise three stories that could stand alone reasonably well, yet still form a cohesive arc. This was an opportunity to bring changes to the status quo, advance the main characters, and introduce new supporting characters.

Tsshar Murieff was a character I've had in mind for a long time (though not under that exact name), inspired by my beloved tabby cat Natasha (1991-2008), and I've tried to incorporate her into one or two other unsold projects before finding a good home for her here. Meanwhile, I'd always intended to give David a love interest as a rival for Nashira, though I'd assumed it would be a woman. Once I decided to add material in *Hub Space* establishing David as bisexual, I realized I should follow through on that and give him a male lover instead. While I've had a handful of gay or bisexual male characters in my prior fiction, I'd never actually portrayed any of them engaging in an "onscreen" romance as I've done with numerous heterosexual and lesbian characters. I felt that I should remedy that omission, for the sake of being inclusive for my readers and expanding my horizons as a writer. Thus, Julio Rodriguez was born. The choice to make him a scientist/engineer was influenced by the British sitcom *Red Dwarf*, which was able to explore richer science fiction concepts once the character of Kryten was added in the third season to provide exposition and advance stories through his technical expertise. Art, a Fishy Intelligence serves a similar expository function. He's a character I've been trying to work in since "Home is Where the Hub Is" but couldn't find room for until "Hubpoint of No Return."

I managed to get two of the new stories written in 2016 and then got stuck on the third, because I'd rushed into writing it before I really had an ending worked out. But a *Star Trek* novel deadline intervened, and only when that was done could I finally work out how to conclude the Hub trilogy. I made the mistake of submitting all three stories back to back, which made it a tougher decision for *Analog*'s editor Trevor Quachri to weigh, and so it took a lot longer than I'd hoped to sell all three. Particularly since the first draft of the second story was a little too risqué for *Analog* and needed a rewrite before I could sell the latter two. Thus, it ended up taking nearly five years to get new Hub stories into print.

As with the *Hub Space* collection, *Crimes of the Hub* adds new material within and between the stories to flesh things out a bit more, and to offer something new for those who've read the original stories in *Analog*. Last time, I inserted in-universe articles as interludes between the stories, but this time, since the stories were written as a single arc, I decided to add bridging scenes to merge them into a short fix-up novel. The entirety of Chapter 6 and the first scene of Chapter 11 are new to this collection, and there are minor additions or expansions to a few other scenes, including the restoration of a bit of the material I cut from "…And He Built a Crooked Hub." I've also trimmed, rephrased, or consolidated redundant bits of character and backstory exposition. But all the character action, in-story facts, and dialogue are unchanged from the original *Analog* versions, except for the reinsertion of two deleted paragraphs ("How long?" and the response) during David and Nashira's conversation in the first scene of Chapter 9, and a couple of slight changes to the description of Nashira's itinerary and movements in Chapter 8 to correct inconsistencies.

A few acknowledgments: The inspiration for the archive's artificial gravity mechanism was the paper "Homopolar artificial gravity generator based on frame-dragging" by Martin Tajmar (*Acta Astronautica*, Volume 66, Issue 9, p. 1297-1301), along with the Forward catapult concept discussed by Robert L. Forward in his book *Indistinguishable from Magic* (Baen Books, 1995). Forward proposed the device as a starship launcher, but I realized it could be used as an artificial gravity generator in the same way Tajmar proposed for his homopolar generator.

The main inspiration for "...And He Built a Crooked Hub" was Robert A. Heinlein's classic tesseract-home story "—And He Built a Crooked House—", first published in the February 1941 issue of *Astounding Science Fiction*, the precursor to *Analog*. The stateroom sketch in The Marx Brothers' 1935 classic *A Night at the Opera* was the other main inspiration, along with the 1992 bedroom-farce film *Noises Off*, based on the 1982 play by Michael Frayn.

Nashira's Cantonese given name Wai-hing (惠慶) means "kind fortune" or "generous good luck," roughly the equivalent of Nashira, which is Arabic for "bringer of good news" or "fortunate one." Her surname Wing (榮) means glory/honor or to flourish/prosper. Róng Huìqìng is the Mandarin Chinese pronunciation of Wing Wai-hing.

Further story discussion and notes can be found on my website:

https://christopherlbennett.wordpress.com/home-page/original-fiction/hub-space-tales-from-the-greater-galaxy/.

ABOUT THE AUTHOR

Christopher L. Bennett is a lifelong resident of Cincinnati, Ohio, with a B.S. in Physics and a B.A. in History from the University of Cincinnati. A fan of science and science fiction since age five, he has sold original short fiction to magazines such as *Analog Science Fiction and Fact* and *Buzzy Mag* and is one of Pocket Books' most prolific and popular authors of Star Trek tie-in fiction, including the epic Next Generation prequel *The Buried Age*, the ongoing Star Trek: Enterprise—*Rise of the Federation* series, and the Star Trek: *Department of Temporal Investigations* series. His original novel *Only Superhuman*, perhaps the first hard science fiction superhero novel, was voted Library Journal's SF/Fantasy Debut of the Month for October 2012. His homepage and Written Worlds blog can be found at http://christopherlbennett.wordpress.com/, and his Facebook author page is at https://www.facebook.com/ChristopherLBennettAuthor

Curious about other Crossroad Press books?
Stop by our site:
http://store.crossroadpress.com
We offer quality writing
in digital, audio, and print formats.

Made in the USA
Las Vegas, NV
04 June 2023